HIS BURNING DESIRE

SPARKS OF DESIRE

VALERIE TWOMBLY

Copyright © 2016 by Valerie Twombly

All rights reserved.

Edited by The Editing Hall & JRT Editing

Cover by Original Syn

ISBN: 978-1-5323-8105-8

No part of this book may be reproduced in any form or by any electronic or mechanical means, including information storage and retrieval systems, without written permission from the author, except for the use of brief quotations in a book review.

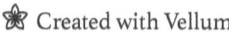 Created with Vellum

ACKNOWLEDGMENTS

The character(s) of [Kate & Ethan] and Dallas Fire & Rescue were created by Paige Tyler for her Dallas Fire & Rescue Series. These elements were used in this work with the author's permission.
https://paigetylertheauthor.com/books/#dallas

1

Connor stood on the ridge, cursing as he stared across the valley and into the gaping mouth of Hell. Fighting fire was his life. His mistress. He had a love-hate relationship with her. The bitch inhaled the pine needles scattered across the ground. A snack served to fuel her burning hunger. Greed sent flames licking up the trees. Some went up in a flash, while others exploded from her fury. She was insatiable.

At least fifty homes filled the landscape in a rural subdivision called Windy Hallow. Aptly named for the breeze that swept through, it kept the residents cool in the summer's heat. Unfortunately, it was those very winds that threatened to destroy the upper class neighborhood.

He moved his attention to his men, who tried to stay ahead of the flames. They'd been furious in their attempts to build a firebreak, dozing a path to the south to keep the fire from spreading back through the forest, which contained thousands of acres of national park. To the east, they were lucky. A river snaked through the park and offered the perfect break. To the west were several miles of rocky terrain. He had men stationed there, but so far, they'd reported the fire had been stopped from spreading in that direction. Now he only had to worry about his men below and the residents. The crew had orders to shift into their dragon and vacate if necessary. Fuck the rules. He'd broken them before, and he'd break them again. The lives of his men came above all else.

In as a team and out as a team. The humans on his crew had witnessed a dragon shift before when things had gotten out of control. Lives had been saved, and that was all that mattered.

He scanned the hillside again. "Stupid fucks," he growled.

Quinn shifted his weight next to him. "Who you referring to?"

Connor didn't break his gaze from the hillside above the homes. The fire was quickly eating up the ground. This year had been unusual, weather-wise. Between the lack of rain, high humidity, heavy winds, and two stupid humans, the blaze was heading for the small community.

"The dumbass kids who thought it might be nice to have a campfire during a red flag warning." He finally turned to look at his partner. "Then not have the fucking balls to report it. Don't their parents teach them about this shit?" Had authorities known earlier, they may have been able to contain the beast.

Quinn scrunched his brows together. "It's taught in school. Every child learns about forest fires at a young age in these parts. Did they find them yet?"

"Yep. Took Sanders all of ten seconds to pinpoint where the fire started and follow the scent of the two boys responsible." It had been reported that the teens had gone white as a sheet when Sanders had shown up at their door with the authorities. Connor wasn't surprised since the shifter was intimidating. At six-six, he was not only tall, but had muscle stacked on muscle. When he opened his mouth to speak, it came out more as a growl. Yet, he was also about as gentle as they came.

The kids' parents tried to deny their sons would be so irresponsible, but dragon shifters didn't make mistakes. Their scenting abilities rivaled that of a bloodhound, a thousand times over.

"Shit." Quinn jerked off his helmet and rubbed his head. "The residents have been evacuated and a structure team called in. How old were the boys?" Of course Quinn would want to know. After all, these were his people. Quinn was one of the few humans allowed to join a shifter wildland crew. He'd proved his worth and had been with them for the last five years.

"Fourteen and sixteen, and don't go getting all sappy, telling me boys do stupid shit." Connor brought his focus back to the smoke-filled sky. "My father would have beat my ass till it was the color of a red-hot poker for something like this."

Quinn shook his head. "I'm not making excuses. What they did was wrong, but they'll have to live with their own guilt." He pulled his heavy coat back on, though the sun seared everything in its path, and the temps spiked to a sweltering ninety-five.

Connor wiped sweat from his brow. Dragons hated heat but loved fire. The tales that they could breathe fire were as far-fetched as pigs flying out of someone's ass. There were a few who could conjure fire using dragon magic, but that was entirely different. He also donned his coat and slapped the helmet back on his head. A splitting ache hammered behind his eyes and into his temples. He liked to think it was stress, but dragons didn't fall to human ailments. No, this was only another telltale sign of something he didn't want to think about.

He was entering the Kamirth. Hell for a male dragon.

Jenna never thought she'd become a pet owner, let alone a cat person. However, the little ball of black fluff purring on her lap had managed to steal her heart. She stroked Buster's fur as she watched her roomie flip through a magazine on the couch across from her.

"I'm bored," Kate sighed.

"So what else is new?" Jenna stared at her roommate, Kate Fairchild. They'd met a year ago when Jenna had come to Dallas to start a new life. She'd walked into Station 58 for her first shift as an EMT, and the two had instantly hit it off. Many of the crew harassed them, asking if they were really sisters. With matching blonde hair, and similar likes and dislikes, the only differences were Kate's green eyes and Jenna's hazel.

After working together a couple of weeks, Kate had lost the lease on her apartment, and Jenna hadn't thought twice about inviting her to come live with her. When she'd moved to Dallas, she'd purchased a brick ranch home with four bedrooms and two full baths that sat on several acres. There was more than enough room while still allowing the girls their privacy.

Kate raised a brow as she peeked over the top of her rag. "I can't help it. We should get dressed up and go out for dinner. Maybe a few drinks after?"

Jenna rolled her eyes. Since she'd moved to Dallas, Kate had been trying to set her up on a date with a rugged-looking fireman named Derrick. She had to admit, she was attracted to him, and they seemed to hit it off. Derrick had been the one to give her the grand tour of the station and fill her in on all the "need to know" about the others who worked there. He'd also been there on her first call, when they were summoned to a fire that had trapped some elderly residents. It had been touch and go for a bit, but everyone got out and survived.

"What are you really up to?"

"Well damn, Jenna. Am I that transparent?" Kate threw on her best smile then tossed the magazine aside. "Derrick keeps asking about you."

Jenna's interest grew. "What kind of questions?"

Her friend leaned forward. "You've never talked about your life back in Minnesota. The only thing I know about you is you're a half dragon shifter with a kick ass ability to be a human MRI."

Jenna responded with a sheepish grin. Yeah, she could touch a person and see inside them. Find broken bones, damaged organs, and even a fatal disease like cancer. If necessary, she could sustain their life until real medical help arrived, but that's where her talent stopped. She couldn't heal them. She always hoped one day she might gain healing powers and not have to rely on conventional human means, but she walked away from that chance when she left Connor.

She would never share his power or anything else, and just thinking about him caused her heart to ache. She tried to forget him. Shove him into the deepest, darkest recesses of her mind, but he proved difficult to forget. Part of her had always hoped he would come searching for her. Tell her how madly in love with her he was, and no matter what they'd be together forever. So far, it hadn't happened.

She shrugged. "Not much to tell really."

"I've heard you have arranged marriages. Is that true?"

How to respond? The elders frowned on sharing too much information about their culture, yet they expected humans to embrace them. It had only been a couple hundred years since dragons had entered society. To say it had been a cluster fuck was mild. Jenna had been a hundred years old at the time. Young for a dragon, what humans would consider their early twenties, and she remembered the fall-out.

The first fifty years had been all out war. It had taken a team from both sides to sit down and talk rationally. Things calmed once humanity realized dragons were not there to take over and could actually be an asset to their society. Occasional extremists tried to cause trouble with outcries of bomb threats or that dragons were going to kill them all and take over the planet. If that had been true, it would have happened eons ago. Dragons had been around since the beginning of time and were far stronger than humans. Instead, they tried to blend in where possible. The elders even forbade shifting, only allowing a dragon flight in the wilds of their secret homeland, where humans were less likely to take notice.

"Jenna? What's it like being a halfling?"

Jenna hid a cringe. She scratched Buster behind the ear and tried to hide how much she hated the word. Hated what she was. "I don't know anything else so that's kinda hard to answer. As far as the arranged marriage? Yes, it's true."

Kate's green eyes widened as did her mouth. "No shit? So does that mean I need to tell Derrick to back off?"

It was at that moment she firmly reminded herself why she'd

moved to Dallas. To begin a new life and it was time she started. "No. I say we get dressed and go have some fun."

Kate jumped to her feet, a big smile plastered on her lips. "Wear something sexy," she hollered as she sped down the hall toward her room. Jenna made a quick mental note of her wardrobe and had the perfect outfit picked out before she even left her chair.

The phone sang out an AC/DC tune in his pocket as Connor shoved open the cabin door. He was dirty, tired, and crankier than fuck, so debated on ignoring the call. Instead, he pulled the annoyance from his pocket and looked at the screen.

His commander.

"Fuck." With a quick swipe, he activated the call to speaker. "Yeah?" He toed off his heavy boots, not caring he left them in the middle of the kitchen floor. He wanted relief. Unfortunately, this wasn't the release he needed. That would require a female either on her knees sucking his cock, or him pounding into her from behind. His balls tightened at the thought.

"O'Rourke. Pack your shit, you're going to Dallas," the voice blared through the speaker as he set the phone on the counter so he could strip.

"For what?" He tried not to let his annoyance bleed through but failed.

"They've had a rash of arsons and requested one of our men. I offered you."

Double fuck! "Can't someone else go?" He pulled his tee over his head and tossed it aside.

"No. The plane leaves at nine pm. Be on it." The phone went silent, and Connor knew his boss had hung up. Command issued, there was no getting out of it. He looked at the clock on the wall. Four hours until he had to leave. Shoving his jeans off, he headed for the shower. Maybe getting the soot and sweat off him would improve his attitude.

Who the fuck am I kidding? he thought as he stepped under the hot spray. He stuck his head into the water and let it soak through his thick hair. Leaning in further, the heat penetrated into his tired muscles. He grabbed a bar of soap and scrubbed. Annoyance ran through him like hot lava when his thoughts turned to her.

Jenna.

The one betrothed to him when he was little more than three hundred years old. She'd been a baby when their fathers had decided the two would be joined. He still recalled the pinprick her father had made on her little finger so he could draw blood for Connor to taste. She hadn't made a peep. And when he'd done the same, placing his finger on her lips, she'd opened and suckled. Their bond had begun; it would be finished when she was old enough to mate.

When his little blonde, hazel-eyed female had started school, he'd watched over her. Making sure she was safe and living the life every child should have. When she entered her teens, he moved away so he didn't have to witness something that might have him wanting to kill someone. Jenna's mother had insisted her daughter go to public high school and hang with other humans. Connor had truly wanted her to live life as any normal girl. He realized how difficult their culture was and how "old world" many of their rules were.

When she celebrated her one-hundredth birthday, he'd come back. He remembered how she had looked at him and the instant recognition in her eyes. He hadn't made demands. Instead, he had begun a relationship like any other man and woman. He hated the old ways and wanted their relationship to go slow. Give her time to acclimate, and above all else, he'd wanted her to fall in love with him.

His cock thickened at the remembrance of her in a string bikini not too long ago. Curves that went forever, covered by a puny piece of red fabric as she lay on the beach. Thank god, they'd been on private property so he hadn't had to kill anyone ogling her. That was the night they'd made love on the sand. Their first time together and she was a perfect fit. It had been the beginning of the end for him, in more ways than one. She'd stolen his heart.

The taste of her lips still sat on his tongue as if he'd kissed her only hours ago rather than close to a year before.

"Shit," he groaned. His palm still lathered from the soap, he reached for his aching member. With a long, slow stroke from root to tip, all while thinking how badly he needed her now, he imagined tangling his fingers in her long locks while he slipped into her heated channel.

He stroked faster.

Would he take her hard and fast? Maybe soft and slow, tearing cries of pleasure from her as he teased her with the head of his cock, penetrating only slightly until she begged him for mercy. In his dreams, her hazel eyes looked up at him and swirled with desire as she wrapped her pink lips around his cock and sucked.

He slapped his free hand on the tile and braced himself. His thighs, a compact mass of muscle, flexed as his breathing grew heavy. He squeezed his shaft harder, pumping into his fist. His wings pressed into the skin on his back, and his bones ached with the urge to shift.

Balls pulling tight, he threw his head back and grunted. His seed hit the black tile, pulse after pulse, until finally he was spent. For the moment, anyway.

He rested his forehead on his arm, knowing this would be one of many times he'd have to give himself release. The Kamirth, a time when a male dragon went into a sexual lust so powerful he'd kill, was closing in on him. Eventually, he would be forced to seek a willing female. Either a full blood or halfling were the only ones who could satiate the Kamirth.

"Damn it, Jenna, why the fuck did you run off?" He wanted the one female meant for him, but she'd made it clear how she felt. And the only thing she'd left behind was a note.

2

Jenna and Kate stepped into The Fargo and headed straight for the bar. A Carrie Underwood tune drifted across the room as the girls took up a saddle fitted as a stool.

"Two amaretto stone sours," Jenna yelled over the music, swaying in her seat as the bartender walked away to make their drinks. Kate gave her a light punch in the arm.

"Look at you. I haven't seen you this relaxed in... Well, ever I believe." She giggled.

The drinks were set in front of them. "Compliments of the gentleman over there." The bartender jerked his head, and Jenna caught sight of Derrick across the room. She had to admit, he caused a flutter in her chest. She smiled, and he tipped the brim of his black cowboy hat and grinned.

Kate raised her glass in a salute to the hotness that was Derrick. "You need to go talk to him. Dancin' wouldn't hurt either."

"I will." She took a sip of the icy drink and licked her lips.

His gaze dropped to her mouth, and she could sense his desire from across the room. A benefit of being a halfling though she often considered it more of an annoyance. Derrick stood and made his way around the large rectangular bar.

Kate smacked her on the arm again. "He's coming this way. I'm going to make my thanks and scoot out of here."

"No! I'm not ready to be alone with him." Panic beat against her ribs. She was good at flirting from afar, but up close and personal? Well, that was a whole different animal. One with teeth and she was afraid it would bite.

"Oh stop. Look at all these people. You're hardly alone."

Before Jenna could reply, Derrick and his six-foot-three-inch frame towered over her.

"Howdy." He grinned and revealed perfect white teeth.

"Derrick, thanks for the drink. Would you think me rude if I left you two alone and went socializing?" Kate asked.

"You're welcome, darlin' and I don't believe you have a rude bone in your body." There was that smile again.

Kate waggled her fingers. "Tootles." Then drifted into a sea of people. Jenna made a mental note to pay her back later.

"Hi, Derrick." Jenna rubbed her sweaty palms on her jeans, suddenly aware of the low cut top she wore. *What the hell was I thinking?* His gaze remained that of a gentleman. On her eyes.

"Evenin', Jenna." He straddled the saddle, his tight jeans revealing muscled thighs. Being a firefighter, he was in great shape. The tight black tee that stretched across his broad chest was proof of it. Women across the bar eyed him with a "take me home and fuck the hell out of me" look. The black hat didn't help matters either. Nor did his baby-blues that sparkled in contrast to his short, raven hair and three-day scruff. If you looked up rugged cowboy, you'd find his picture.

"You on call tonight?" he asked, pulling her from her daze.

"I'm always on call, I thought you knew that." Her special gifts didn't save her from being pulled away from a good time or out of a deep slumber. "I don't mind though, and one drink won't hurt." Her dragon DNA would process alcohol in minutes. Kind of a drag, but she'd known nothing else.

"You are a special one, Jenna." He smiled again.

Her cheeks heated. "It's always good when the phone doesn't ring. Means I'm not needed. I like not being needed."

"Oh, everyone likes to be needed in one way or another." His slight, southern twang made her toes curl. Couple that with a grin that would melt the panties off any woman, and she wanted to run. Far away. Right back into the arms of the man who still held her heart no matter how hard she tried to forget him.

She shifted. "I suppose."

He swigged his beer and swallowed, wiping the back of his hand across his mouth. "I can't believe shifters are any different."

She averted her gaze to the rim of her glass. "I'm not a shifter. I'm a halfling. My father is a dragon and my mother human."

"I see. I'm curious then, if a dragon lives for thousands of years, isn't it rather heartbreaking to lose those they love? They do love, right?"

"Of course we do. My mother and father love each other very much. It's a bond unlike any other. When they mated, my mother took some of my father's power, which also extends her life. At least for as long as he lives."

Derrick rubbed his jaw. "Wow, that's pretty cool. So tell me, if you mate with a dragon, will you gain more power? How long does a halfling live?"

Jenna shook her head. "You're just full of questions, aren't you?" She swore if the room was brighter, she would've seen him blushing.

"Sorry, I guess that is kinda rude of me. I certainly didn't mean to be nosy." He looked away, picked up his beer, and took another swig.

"Hey, I didn't mean it that way." She glanced down at the floor then back up at him. "I tend to keep to myself and forget that people are curious." A fast-paced song pounded a beat out over the speakers, and she had the sudden urge to dance. "Do you like to dance?"

His eyes lit up and that sexy grin returned. "You bet." They both pushed off their saddles at the same time, feet hitting the floor, and he extended his hand. As soon as she placed her palm in his, butterflies bounced in her stomach.

Her phone went off.

"Damm it, that's the station calling."

Connor stared out the window of the private jet as he settled into the leather seat. Nothing much to see, except darkness. The weather from northern Minnesota to Dallas was expected to be calm. He grunted then stared at the folder on the table next to him. The red file contained all the information Dallas authorities had on the arsons.

The first fire started in the basement of an abandoned building. The only reason investigators knew it was arson was the accelerant used. If whoever started the fire had not used gasoline, they might have gotten away with it. The building, occupied only by the homeless, was full of garbage. Mattresses, torn up couches, blankets, and clothing along with trash littered the place, especially the basement. It was obvious whoever had done this had been seeking a thrill. The "high," firefighters called it. Fortunately, no one had been seriously injured or killed.

The second had been identical to the first. Again, another abandoned building within the city. This, too, had started in the basement. Gasoline seemed to be the favored accelerant. Unfortunately, this had been a four-story building, which stood in an older industrial neighborhood where several other structures were no longer being used. The ones that were still occupied had been closed down for the night. There had been no one around to call 9-1-1 for help. It was only when a resident a few miles away spotted the black smoke, that someone made the call. By the time firefighters arrived on the scene, there hadn't been much left. Authorities suspected it was started by the same person. However, they couldn't rule out a copycat.

The third fire had started in the stairs but this time in a small apartment building. Two floors, with ten apartments total. An elderly couple and their cat had died from the smoke. Authorities now believed they had not only a murderer, but a serious arsonist on their hands.

The fourth, and so far the last fire had been slightly different. In their usual MO, the fire was started in the basement. This time the arsonist targeted a single-family home in a neighborhood where houses stood within feet of each other. Not only had he or she decided to break in and burn down a family's house, they wanted to see the whole neighborhood go up. A trail of gasoline had gone from the starting point to the house next door, where the assailant had doused the bushes that nestled up to the siding. Another trail led across the small backyard to the house in the back. It appeared the son of a bitch was playing connect the dots. However, they had stopped there. Whether it was because they ran out of fuel or feared getting caught, it was uncertain. No one had seen a thing.

Connor rubbed his temples as the pilot announced they were beginning their descent for landing. They should be in Dallas in about twenty minutes. From there, he'd take a car straight to Station 58 where he was supposed to meet with the captain and a local detective. He closed the folder, shoved it into his bag, and did a quick check of his email before logging off. As he went to shut down his laptop, he took a second to look at the last photo he'd taken of Jenna before she ran off. Hazel eyes haunted him as they stared back, and he wondered what he'd done that had caused her to leave. A glutton for misery, he reached into the black leather bag and pulled out a worn envelope. The one that contained her last words. Unfolding the paper, he read what he already knew by heart.

Connor,

I'm so sorry to let you down. I realize a letter is so impersonal, but it is better this way. I'm leaving. Please don't try and find me. My parents won't even know where I am, only that I'm safe. I need to start a new life, one that doesn't include us being together. It's nothing you did, it's me and always has been. You've been great, but you deserve better than me.

Break the bond and find someone who makes you happy.

Regards,
Jenna

Apparently, she failed to realize that *she* had been the one to make him happy. Had he scared her off somehow? As he'd done every day since she'd left, he retraced their last night together, a little more than a year ago now. He'd invited her for dinner at his place and cooked her favorite. Steak, medium-rare with baked potato and green beans fresh from the garden. For dessert, chocolate ice cream with strawberries. She'd eaten every bite.

Later, they'd sat on the back deck in a swing he'd built the summer before, holding hands, and watched the sun set. As the sky lit with vibrant colors of pink and orange, he'd gotten down on one knee and proposed. Even though they had already started a bond when she was but a babe, he wanted to make things official. He wanted to cater to her human side by presenting her with a three-karat diamond. Promised to buy her any wedding dress she wanted and they could have a ceremony with all the human frills on the date of her choosing. He only asked that they complete the bonding ritual of the dragon shortly after.

Her hesitation should have been a dead giveaway something was amiss, but when he'd asked, she denied anything was wrong. The next evening, her parents had come to him with the note and the ring. They swore they had no idea where she'd gone and thought she just needed some time to think. He reluctantly agreed. That had been a year ago. Jenna would have recently celebrated her three hundredth birthday, and he had missed it.

City lights came into view as they approached the airport. He buckled his seatbelt and prepared for landing, his thoughts still on Jenna. He needed to push that female to the recesses of his mind, so he could track the arsonist and get the hell out of Dallas. City life had never been something he liked. Open skies, clean air, and forested land was where he was most comfortable. There was another reason for wanting to close up this case and be on his way. He was going to search for his mate. It was past time for answers as to why she left.

The plane came to a halt, and as soon as the door opened, he descended the stairs. Air so thick and hot, wrapped around him and squeezed. It reminded him of the fire he'd just fought. He'd never been to Dallas but already he hated it.

He strode across the private runway, heading for the pickup truck that sat near the hangar. He would have much preferred a Harley, but this was more suited to the business at hand. Perhaps later, he'd have time to grab a bike and go for a ride. He pulled open the door, tossed his bag across the seat, and climbed in. Searing heat crawled down his spine, curled around his torso, and made a beeline for his balls.

"Damn." Apparently, the heat was also affecting the Kamirth because he had a sudden urge to fuck. He might have to check out one of the local clubs and find him a willing female. At this point, he could still sleep with a human and gain a little relief. However, later he would require one of his own.

3

Jenna stepped outside the club and pulled out her phone to read the text message. Derrick slipped up behind her.

"What's going on?" Concern laced his voice.

She quickly read the text. "There's an accident not far from here. I've got to go." She looked around and realized driving was out of the question, since it would take her longer to get there than it would on foot. Plus, Kate had driven and had the keys. "Shit." She muttered under her breath, regretting she was unable to shift. She quickly pulled off the high heels she wore and shoved them at Derrick. "Here, hold on to these." Before he could respond, she took off at a high-speed sprint down the sidewalk.

"Wait!" Derrick yelled, but Jenna was already too far away to hear anything else he shouted. Maybe she couldn't shift, but she could run faster than any ordinary human. She only hoped it was fast enough.

Four blocks later, she spotted the flashing red lights as she closed in on them. By her calculations, she should only be about a block away. Reaching deep inside for an extra burst of speed, she pushed forward and ignored the growing blisters on the bottoms of her feet. They would heal after a good soak. As she rounded the corner, she finally spotted the carnage. Twisted metal that was now unrecognizable filled the street. Police, firefighters, and paramedics hustled through the scene, and she wasn't sure which way to go.

"Over here," someone yelled, and she headed in the direction of the voice she recognized as belonging to Trent, a fellow paramedic.

She dropped to her knees beside him and peered inside the wreckage. The lights, setup to help rescuers see their grisly work, revealed way too much blood. The woman was pinned. Twisted metal stuck into her chest, and it was hard to tell if it went straight through or not. She reached between a small opening of glass and metal and touched the woman whose eyes flitted open. Jenna saw death lingering in them before she even began her scan.

"S-save my baby." Her chest rattled.

"She's not going to make it. We have others who need our help, but she keeps talking about her baby. We've searched but can't find anyone," Trent said.

It was at that moment Jenna sensed a small flutter. She probed deeper, her gift allowing her to see inside the woman's body. "Damn. She's eight months pregnant. You can't tell with all the wreckage blocking her belly."

"We need to get her out. Can you hold both of them?" Trent didn't wait for a reply. He jumped to his feet and began yelling commands to those nearby.

Jenna shoved her ability into high gear and scanned the mother's internal organs. She was pinned at the chest, but her stomach had somehow been protected. The baby grew weaker by the minute, and mom had lost a lot of blood. Jenna closed her eyes. "You need to hurry, Trent." Sustaining more than one life would drain her fast. Once again, she cursed under her breath and wished she'd been born a full dragon.

A faint heartbeat drummed in her ears. She summoned every ounce of power available to her and wrapped invisible fingers around both the mother and child. Their life forces held to her, taking from her own. Jenna had to shove back anger and disappointment in herself. If she could have shifted, she would've made it here faster. Seconds might have made a difference in helping the mother.

"It's a girl," she whispered as someone dropped in next to her. She opened her eyes. "Derrick. I wasn't expecting you."

He studied her. "You look pale. Trent went to see if anyone else needed help"

She forced a smile. Just like him to be concerned about her welfare. "Tell them to hurry." She felt herself sway, and the drone of machinery rang faintly in her ears.

"Jesus, Jenna. You don't look well." He touched her arm. "You're burning up. What's going on?"

"I-I don't have enough power to keep them both alive. The mother is draining me, and my body is overheating. I can't hold onto her much longer. If I lose consciousness, I'll lose the baby too."

"Then you have to let the mom go. We can't help her, but her daughter stands a chance." His hands cupped each side of her face. "Do you hear me, Jenna? Let her go."

Tears blurred her vision further as she let the woman's life force slip away. The sound of shredding metal stopped and yelling ensued.

The mother's heart stopped.

"Jenna, they have her free. You're going to have to stand up. Let me help." Derrick put his arm around her waist, and she slumped into him.

"Okay but I can't break contact or I lose the baby."

How they managed, she had no idea since everything was a blur, but they'd gotten the woman free and onto a stretcher. It appeared the rescuers had cut the chunk that had impaled the woman as close to her body as they dared. Jenna walked alongside with Derrick's assistance as the paramedics wheeled the victim toward the ambulance. Once inside, they wasted no time in heading to the nearest hospital. The paramedic across from her in the ambulance called in to announce they were coming and to relay the details of the accident. A team would be standing by waiting to perform a cesarean section and offer life support to the baby if necessary. Jenna would have no choice but to keep hold of the infant's life force, until the doctors were able to remove the baby from the mother's womb. She was now this child's only link to survival.

As the ambulance made its way across the city, she could feel Trent's gaze on her. "How's the baby doing?"

"She's hanging in there."

"I don't know how you do it, but I'm glad you're here." He slapped a cuff on her arm to check her blood pressure. "Will it help if I give you an IV?"

"No." She finally lifted her gaze to meet his, feeling as tired as she imagined she looked. "I didn't make it in time, and now this little girl will have to grow up without her mother."

His gaze softened. "We can't save everyone and you know that."

Her jaw tensed. "If I could've shifted, I would've made it."

"You saw her insides. Tell me she could have been saved."

He was right. The steel had punctured both lungs and nicked the heart. By all rights, she should have been dead when Jenna arrived. Sheer determination of a mother had kept her breathing. Her thoughts moved back to Connor. He was a powerful dragon and had she mated him, she may have been able to save the woman. The thought only worsened her guilt. She should have stayed and faced whatever challenges came her way. Instead, she ran from the man she loved.

"What about the others? Any survivors?" She closed her eyes again and focused on the baby. The little girl was a fighter.

"The semi driver had minor injuries as far as we could tell. I think he'll be okay." At that moment, the ambulance stopped and the back doors swung open. A nurse issued orders as the driver came around and assisted Trent in getting the stretcher out and rolling through the emergency room. They were directed behind a curtain where a team was standing by ready to go.

A doctor tied his mask. "You have been keeping the baby alive?"

Jenna nodded. "She has a steady heartbeat." She moved her hand along the woman's side and down her leg until she was touching the ankle.

"We need you to gown up," said a nurse next to her, holding out a gown. Jenna quickly shoved her arm into the hole then switched hands. By the time they had a mask on her, the doctor had already started making his incision.

"I'll need to know before you cut the cord," she blurted out. The team all looked at her with questioning eyes. "I'm sharing my life force with her, using the umbilical cord. An abrupt break might hurt us both."

What felt like minutes ticked by until the infant was lifted from the protection of the womb. The last connection the little girl would ever have with her mother ended, and Jenna experienced a rush of sadness. A nurse suctioned the baby's nose and mouth, and the room filled with relief as she let out her first cry. This time, Jenna let her tears fall. Miracles really did happen. She lifted her hand from the mother's leg, disconnecting herself from the baby.

"You can cut the cord anytime."

Connor drove along the expressway, following the instructions of the annoying voice on the GPS. When the lady in the box announced to take the next exit, he signaled and got off the interstate. Making his way down quiet city streets, he promptly hit a traffic jam.

"Good Lord, this is some messed up shit." He wondered if it was normal to hit traffic so late at night. He spotted an officer heading down the line of cars in front of him, stopping at each one for a moment to speak to the driver. When he approached, Connor hit the switch to lower his window.

"Evening, officer."

The man nodded his head. "Evening, where you headed?"

"Station 58, I have some business there."

"Bad accident up the road and it's gonna take them a bit to clear it out. You can turn left up here at the next street." He pointed. "Go a couple of blocks to the light then take a right. You'll see the station from there."

Connor noted the vehicles in front of him were pulling into the other lane and traveling up to the next intersection. "I'll do that. Thanks, I hope there were no casualties." The officer had already moved on to the car behind him, so he pulled out and followed the traffic.

Once he'd gotten onto Fisk Ave, the annoying woman started blurting out directions. Finally, he took a right at the light, and there he could actually see the fire station. He pulled into the lot, shoved the truck in park, and jumped out. Sweat immediately trickled down the back of his neck, and he swore before he spun, making a complete circle. Something familiar touched him. Was it possible Jenna had been here? Why did he feel her all around him? It was as if she were both in the station and down the street.

He scrubbed his face. He really was losing it.

Connor strode across the pavement and through the open overhead door, stopping in front of the first person he spotted.

"Names Connor, I'm looking for Detective Collins."

A young man jerked his head to the right. "He's in the kitchen having coffee."

"Thanks." He headed in the direction the kid indicated. When he stepped through the door, he overheard a conversation about what he guessed was the accident. A semi versus a car. Something about a pregnant woman who died, but the baby was saved by a shifter? He'd have to remember to inquire later about this shifter. Could it be Jenna? He shouldn't get his hopes up.

Finally, all conversation stopped and eyes turned to him. A guy in a pair of jeans and a button-down navy blue shirt jumped to his feet and rounded the table.

"Hi, you must be Connor, I'm Ethan Collins." He held out his hand; Connor accepted and gave a firm shake. "Would you like some coffee?"

"Sure, I'd love a cup. Cream, please." He pulled out a chair and took a seat across from two other firefighters. Ethan set the coffee down in front of him and took the seat to his left.

"So I hear you're one of the best around," the blond across from him stated.

Connor lifted the cup of coffee. "I am, and I'm curious. You mentioned having a shifter on your crew. What's their name?"

"That would be Jenna Dunne. I sure hope you can help us catch this person," Ethan said.

Connor's chest tightened, and he had to set his cup back on the table before he splashed coffee everywhere.

An alarm went off and an announcement requesting backup. The two guys on the other side of the table jumped to their feet and ran from the room. Ethan shook his head. "Every time I hear that damn thing, I cringe."

"Worried it might be him again?" Connor managed to regain his composure.

"Always. Do you think we're looking for a male suspect?" Ethan ran his thumb over the rim of his coffee cup.

"Usually is. Women aren't much into starting fires. So, tell me. How long has this Jenna been employed here?"

Ethan seemed to contemplate his remark before replying. "About a year, maybe. You know her?"

"Possibly." He wasn't ready to admit he knew exactly who she was.

A cell phone rang. "Excuse me." Ethan pulled the phone from his back pocket. "Yeah."

Connor was in tune to the man's body language. A slight stiffening of the jaw indicated the news on the other end wasn't pleasant. When the detective finally hung up, Connor had already surmised what the conversation was about.

"Let me guess, our man has struck again?"

Ethan jumped to his feet. "I don't know if this is our guy, but the house was fully engulfed when our crew arrived. The neighbors say a young woman lives in the house alone, and they last saw her when she came home from work around five. She would have been asleep by now, and no one can find her."

Connor wasted no time getting to his feet. "You drive." He was heading out the door before the other man could even reply.

4

Jenna tore off her mask and looked at herself in the mirror. "Damn, I look like shit."

"You did a great job." Jenna was so run down, she hadn't even noticed when one of the nurses slid in beside her at the sink. "The baby's father is with her now." She shook her brown curls. "Tears of sadness and happiness all in one."

"How is the little one?"

"Everything checked out great. She's one lucky little girl." The nurse flashed a smile. "She's in the nursery if you want to take a peek."

Jenna looked back at her reflection. "I might slip up there before I go." She felt a light touch on her shoulder.

"Make sure you get some rest soon." The nurse turned and left the room.

Jenna splashed cold water on her face, grabbed a towel, and dried off. She stepped from the room and headed to the bank of elevators. When the doors finally opened, she was relieved to discover it empty, so she stepped in and jabbed the button for the third-floor. It was then she realized she didn't have any shoes on, only the little booties the nurses had given her. The doors slid open and she walked out, turned to the right, and headed toward the nursery. Thankfully, it was late, and there were not a lot of people around because she wasn't in the mood to be social.

As she stepped to the window, she spotted a man sitting in a rocking chair, holding a tiny bundle. Instantly, she knew it was the little girl. A nurse walked by on the other side of the glass and tapped the gentleman on the shoulder. When he looked up at her, the woman pointed toward the window. Jenna couldn't make out what they were saying, but she had a feeling it was about her. When he looked her way, his eyes lit up. He rose from the chair and walked toward her. Stopping at the glass in front of her, he pulled the blanket aside so she could get a better look at the baby.

He smiled at her, and mouthed the words "thank you."

She pressed both palms against the glass. "You're welcome."

He moved and pointed to a bassinet that held a little sign that said, "My name is Hope." Tears stung her eyes, but she held them back. "That's a beautiful name." She waved her fingers. "Have to go now." Before he could respond, she sped away from the window and back down the hall toward the elevator. The door opened as soon as she hit the button, and she practically leapt inside. She pressed herself against the back wall, closed her eyes, and lost her battle with the tears that streaked down her cheeks.

Her thoughts quickly moved to Connor and the life she desperately wanted for them to have together. Her heart broke all over again at the thought of the one man she tried so hard not to give her heart to. Jenna wanted to be brave. She wanted to believe she could be the perfect mate for him. However, being a halfling meant she stood a good chance of never carrying a dragon child. According to elder law, Connor would be within his rights, and strongly encouraged, to break their bond and find another mate.

She wasn't willing to risk Connor's rejection, so she had fled Minnesota. Left everyone she knew and loved behind to start a new life here in Dallas. All of her emotions, her feelings for Connor, had been buried deep and covered up with her new existence. However, seeing that baby ripped the lid off her well-hidden emotions.

The elevator stopped and the doors opened. Jenna quickly scooted out and headed for the lobby, wiping her tear-stained face.

"Damn it." It dawned on her that she had no ride home. She looked at a clock as she walked past. Midnight. She supposed she could call Kate but hated to interrupt her evening. There was always a cab.

Her stomach growled, breaking her train of thought. The night had taken a lot out of her, and she was starving. Her body begged for sustenance. She crossed the lobby, head down, searching through her phone for a local taxi.

"Jenna."

Startled, she stopped and looked toward the voice. Derrick stood there with a cup of coffee in one hand, and the pair of shoes she handed off to him earlier in the other. She had no idea what to say.

He strode toward her. "I knew you'd need a ride." He gave her a sheepish grin. "And I thought you might need some coffee."

Maybe it was because she was exhausted and starving. Or perhaps it was his simple act of kindness, but she burst into tears again.

"Damn. I didn't mean to upset you."

She shook her head. "No, it's not you. It's been a tough night, and the fact that you even thought of me... Well, I don't know what to say but thank you." She accepted the shoes and moved to a nearby chair. Pulling off the booties, she slipped on her heels and stood, trying not to wince at the pain in her feet. She then accepted the coffee and took a sip, savoring her favorite flavor of butter pecan.

"How did you know this was my favorite?" Connor had known all of her favorites too. *Damn it, I need to stop thinking about him and move on.*

There was that sexy grin again. "I pay attention." He tilted his head. "Are you hungry?"

"I am famished."

"Come on then, let me buy you something to eat. I'll not take no for an answer."

She'd planned to go home and just make a sandwich then fall into bed, but a hot meal did sound a lot better. "I'd like that."

The second Ethan pulled up to the scene, Connor jumped out of the car and stepped next to the chief on command. "Holy hell." The fire had been beaten back, but there was a lot of damage to the front of the house. Fortunately, the homes on either side had been protected and sustained minor to no damage.

"Do we know if anyone was home?" He prayed the answer would be no because there was no way anyone survived this.

"They're still searching, though the neighbors say they saw the woman who lives here come home. Her car is still parked in the garage."

Connor's gaze went to where the garage should have been, and in its place were the skeletal remains of a vehicle. Things weren't looking good. One of the firefighters approached.

"Captain, they found a body."

"Where?" Connor blurted out before the captain could pose the question himself.

The man shuffled his feet, and his gaze darted between Connor and his captain. "We found her in the closet. Gagged and bound."

The captain pulled off his hat and wiped his arm across his brow. "Thanks, Dan." He looked toward Connor. "I'd say we now have a murder."

Connor scratched his chin as he focused on what remained of the structure. "Agreed. People just don't end up that way."

Most of the fire was out and only embers glowed in the darkness. His vision, better than any human, zeroed in on the back of the house. He moved across the property and around to the back, where he could get a close up view of the bedroom.

Ethan followed him.

"The fire didn't start back here," Connor stated. "There's less damage to this part of the house." He peered through a broken window and spotted the victim. The fire hadn't touched her. It was likely if she wasn't already dead, then the smoke had killed her. Connor inhaled sharply. Scents he recognized as those already on the scene filtered through his sensitive nose. The smell of gasoline also assured him it was likely their suspect.

"I don't like the feeling I'm getting here," Ethan stated, standing next to him.

"Neither do I," Connor replied. "Every instinct I possess tells me she knew her assailant."

"Why's that?" The detective coughed as pungent smoke still billowed from the burning embers inside.

He shook his head. "Can't explain it. I also can't detect a scent from anyone not already here." He faced Ethan. "So everyone is now a suspect. I want on this site first thing in the morning." He started to walk away. "Also, can you get me some background information on the woman that lived here?"

Ethan nodded. "I'm on it right now." He pulled his phone from his pocket and started punching the pad as he followed Connor. More police arrived and began marking off the scene. He stopped for a moment and again searched the smells but it was useless. Maybe morning would bring more answers.

Connor turned back and headed toward the car, where he caught up with the detective. "Soon as you're ready, I could use a ride back to my truck. I'll head over to my hotel, but the minute you have any information, don't hesitate to give me a call."

"You got it."

5

Jenna waited while Derrick rounded the truck then opened her door and helped her out. Taking her arm, he led her across the sidewalk and into the little diner named Mel's Place.

"How about a booth in the back?" he asked.

"Perfect." Too tired to care where they sat, she just wanted something to eat and the comfort of her bed.

They headed for the back corner, even though the place was fairly empty and they had their choice of places to sit. She slid across the red vinyl and settled in. Grabbing a menu from a chrome holder, she flipped it open and scanned the items. "Hmm, breakfast, lunch, or dinner?" She glanced at the clock on the wall; it was now closing in on one in the morning. It didn't really matter what she ate as long as it was something.

"You have whatever you want and as much as you need." Derrick looked up from his menu.

The waitress sauntered over, pad in hand, and pulled a pencil from behind her ear. "You guys want coffee?"

"None for me, thanks," Jenna replied.

"Me neither." Derrick looked back at his menu. "You go first."

"I'll have some iced tea, a cheeseburger with everything except onions, and an order of fries." She closed her menu and stuck it back in the holder.

"And you, sir?"

"I'll have the same."

The waitress scratched on her pad then smiled. "Coming right up." She headed off to the counter to place their order.

"It's been a tough evening for you, hasn't it?" Derrick asked as he reached across the table and rubbed his thumb over her knuckles. Her first instinct was to pull away. She'd not let another man touch her since Connor, but she was too tired to move. Plus, the contact felt nice.

"Yes it has. I think this was one of the toughest calls I've ever taken." She finally pulled her hand free and settled both of them in her lap as she stared across the diner. A strange feeling came over her. A feeling of...déjà vu? Not as if she'd been here before, but something was definitely familiar.

She suddenly felt uncomfortable. Like a schoolgirl on a first date, even though this wasn't a date. Or was it? It couldn't be. Derrick was a coworker who was being considerate. They'd been friends since she showed up at the station on her first day. Yes, he was handsome and kind, but could they be more than friends? He'd hinted on several occasions maybe they could. Perhaps it was time she thought about dating again. Maybe that was exactly what she needed to finally get Connor out of her system and move on with her life.

"You look deep in thought."

She gave a slight shrug of her shoulder. "I suppose I drifted away for a moment. That was rude, I'm sorry."

The waitress placed two glasses of ice tea in front of them. "Your food will be up shortly."

"Thanks," Derrick replied with a smile before he focused on Jenna again. "Don't worry about it. Can I ask where you went to?"

"Nowhere, really. Just tired I guess." She brushed a lock of hair from her face. "Thanks for everything. You're a good friend."

"I'd like to be more than your friend, Jenna."

She chewed her bottom lip and contemplated how to respond.

Luckily, the waitress showed up with their food. Jenna inhaled deeply and reached for the ketchup. "God that smells good." Squirting a big puddle on her plate, she ran a fry through it then popped it in her mouth. "It tastes even better."

Derrick chuckled. "If that's not enough for you, you can have some of mine too."

She picked up her burger and grease ran down her wrist. "I think I'll be good with this." Then she shoved the sandwich into her mouth.

Connor jumped into his truck with a promise from the detective he would dig up any information about the woman he could find. Immediately, his thoughts turned to Jenna. She was here, he was sure of it.

As he drove from the fire station lot, his stomach growled, and he realized he hadn't eaten since breakfast. "Siri, find me the closest place to eat." His phone gave him directions to one that wasn't far from his hotel. He made a right at the light and headed down the quiet street until he saw the sign for Mel's Place. Perfect. Looked like the kind of greasy spoon his gut needed. He found a parking space a few slots down and pulled in. When he exited the truck, something caught his attention. His muscles bunched at the familiar scent. It was like a slice of heaven, so he followed it. A low rumble echoed off the side of the building, and he realized it came from him.

He'd been growling.

He glanced around. The sidewalk was empty, as it should be this time of the night, so he stalked forward. When he was in front of the glass door, he stopped and inhaled again.

"It can't be." Had he finally found her? One thing was for sure, he wasn't going to stand outside on the sidewalk and debate with himself. He grabbed the handle, took another deep breath, and pulled open the door. As he stepped inside, he knew for certain he was in the right place. Her scent was so strong, his cock twitched with desire. He did a quick scan of the room. A young couple, likely college-age, sat in a booth close to the door. A middle-aged man sipped coffee at the counter. Connor narrowed his gaze on the booth back in the corner. There was no mistaking Jenna, and she was with another man. Jealousy raged through him.

Mine.

He rolled his fingers into his palms and tried not to growl out loud. Instead, he walked toward her as if he didn't have a care in the world.

Her head snapped up, and her gaze — hazel eyes — met his. Those luscious lips, the ones he'd kissed so long ago, fell open. She tried to hide the surprise on her face but failed miserably. Within seconds, his boots carried him to her table where he stopped in front of her. So many things he wanted to say but where to start?

"So, you leave me for him?" He jerked his head at the guy sitting across from her. It took every ounce of strength not to grab him by the throat and choke the living shit out of him.

"It's not what you think." She shifted in her seat.

The woman had no idea what he thought or what swirled around in his mind right now. The pictures his active imagination conjured were of things she might be doing with this jerk, and a red haze dropped over his vision. However, he wasn't so blind to not notice the dark circles under her eyes and her pale complexion. She was unwell. Either that or this asshole was mistreating her, for which he'd have to kill him.

"Well, sweetheart, what exactly am I thinking?"

"Jenna, who is this guy?" the jerk across from her questioned.

She licked her lips, cast her gaze down at the table, and played with a french fry. "My fiancé."

Jerk face nearly choked. "You didn't tell me you were engaged." The guy slid out from the booth, stood, and stuck out his hand. "Hey, name is Derrick. Jenna and I work together."

Okay, not what he was expecting from Jenna's boyfriend, and he debated grabbing the man's hand and crushing every bone in it. Instead, he did the right thing. Accepted the handshake and gave a nod of acknowledgment. "Connor. Nice to meet you. You one of the firefighters?"

Derrick sat back down. "Yeah, I am."

Connor was taken by surprise when Jenna slid over. "You're welcome to join us." She jabbed another fry into the ketchup and shoved it in her mouth. He wasn't going to let this opportunity slip by, so he moved in beside her. His thigh touched hers, and he let her warmth seep into him. Christ, maybe that was the wrong thing to do. Her heat had him wanting to pin her to the seat. Kiss her until they were both breathless.

"So where you from?" Derrick asked.

"Up north. Minnesota to be exact." He looked over at Jenna, who continued to ignore him and shovel food into her face. "I got called down here to help investigate some arsons."

A look of surprise flashed across Derrick's face. "Really? Is that a specialty of yours?"

Connor rested his arms on the table and leaned in slightly, the need for posturing took over his common sense. "You could say that. I'm a shifter, so I'm pretty damn good at tracking."

Jenna stopped mid-bite and turned to look at him. "Yes, you're an excellent tracker. It says a lot about you." She looked away and went back to eating. Her tone cut like a double-edge sword, and he wished he knew what the hell she'd meant by it.

6

Jenna wasn't sure if she wanted to scream or hit him. Part of her was glad to see him. The other half was full of fear. She was afraid he wouldn't give her what she wanted. Then again, she was so damn confused being near him. She wanted him to give her up, break their bond. She longed for him, desired him to pull her into his arms and kiss her. Tell her how much she meant to him. However, she doubted he'd do any of that. Her statement about him being a good tracker was accurate. If he had really wanted to find her, he could've done so with relative ease. Showing up a year later told her he hadn't wanted to locate her. Maybe by now he'd found someone new. For some reason, the thought nearly crushed her. She shoved it aside. Jenna would get over him if it was the last thing she did.

"Actually, I'm glad to see you, we have some things we need to discuss," she stated.

He refused to look at her, and damn she wished he would move his thigh away from her. "Yes. Yes, we have lots to talk about." The tension rolled off him, and she was grateful that Derrick — being human — wouldn't feel it.

The waitress strolled over. "Sir, can I get you anything?"

"No, I seemed to have lost my appetite," Connor replied.

"What about you two, can I get you anything else?"

"Jenna? You need more food? Something else to drink?" Derrick asked.

She shook her head. "No, I'm fine, thank you." She shoved the last bite of her burger into her mouth and tried to ignore both men. She couldn't remember a time when she'd felt more uncomfortable, but she refused to let this get the better of her.

"Derrick, thanks so much for helping me out tonight. Connor and I need to talk, so you wouldn't mind if he gives me a ride home?"

"Not at all." Derrick put his focus on Connor. "She rescued an unborn infant tonight. Unfortunately, the mother was lost."

Connor looked at her. "I'm sorry. Had I known you needed help..." He drifted off. One thing about Connor, he would know how much she hurt right now. He'd always understood her; he just never loved her.

"I understand there was no helping the mother," Derrick responded. He slid out from his seat. "I'll take care of the check and head home. See you at the station, Jenna. Connor, it was nice meeting you, and I'm sure we'll run into each other again."

"I'm sure we will, and thanks for taking care of Jenna."

Jenna waited until Derrick had paid the bill and walked out before she turned to Connor and glared. If she could make arrows shoot from her eyes, she would pin him to his seat.

"Let's not start our discussion here. I'll drive you home," he growled as he stood and held out his hand to help her. She refused, of course, and pulled her way out of the booth.

Walking next to Connor to the door, she caught the waitress staring at him. A tinge of jealousy ripped through her, but she reminded herself she had been the one to walk away from their relationship. He was free to pursue any woman he wanted. Not that she could blame the other female. After all, Connor stood a good six feet five and had muscles stacked on top of each other. His eyes were the richest brown she'd ever seen. Add to it the scruff on his face, the tight as hell tee he wore, and the *oh so sexy she wanted to trace every line* dragon tattoo on his right bicep. It brought her right back to their last night together. She licked her lips remembering what lie beneath his clothes.

Damn it! Heat ran straight to her core.

Connor opened the door to his truck and helped Jenna inside. Touching her made his jeans so fucking tight it was painful. His mood soured, and he realized his Kamirth drew even closer.

Just fucking wonderful.

He'd suspected it was his Jenna who was the shifter they referred to at the station and thought he was prepared to see her. He'd been dead wrong. How the hell was he going to keep his mind on his duties and still face the woman who'd ripped his heart to shreds?

He climbed into the driver's seat and started the truck. "I'm pretty sure I drove by the accident you were at tonight."

"Oh?"

"You could have reached out for me, and I would have helped you." They had started to develop a telepathic link before she left. After she'd gone, she'd slammed the door on that too.

"How was I to know you were here?" Her tone was void of any emotion; she simply sounded tired, but damn it. Didn't she realize he could have channeled his power through her? However, that wouldn't have been necessary. He'd been here, only blocks away. He would have broken the elder rules and shifted if that's what it would have taken to get to her.

"I guess you wouldn't." He simply left it at that and resumed silence.

She muttered directions. Otherwise, they both remained quiet.

As promised, a few miles down the road she had him turn off onto a gravel drive. He followed the twisting, turning lane until it revealed a brick ranch home at the end. He was immediately impressed with her taste in houses, but quickly reminded himself he was not happy with her. He pulled the truck up by the garage, killed the ignition, and hopped out. Before he could round to the other side, she had the door open and was out of the truck.

"It's late, and I'm tired. How about if we talk later," Jenna stated.

Oh, he was not about to let her brush him off again. "So you can try and disappear again? I don't think so." He watched, rather amused at the irritation on her face.

"Fine." She slammed his truck door and headed toward the house. "I have no idea if my roommate is home or not, so we'll need to keep it down."

Suddenly he had visions of her screaming, naked body beneath him, and he followed like a panting puppy. Pushing open the door, she escorted him across ceramic tile. His boots made enough noise to wake the dead. So much for a possible, sleeping roommate.

"So, is this roommate of yours male or female?"

She stopped abruptly, spun, and faced him. "Screw you."

"I don't get it, Jenna. What the hell did I do to piss you off? Where did I go wrong?"

She tossed her purse on the kitchen table then flipped on a light over the sink. "We're just not going to work, Connor. You need to forget about me, move on, and break the bond we have already."

He leaned against the counter, arms crossed over his chest. "That is not a valid answer. So unless you can give me a real good reason, it's not happening."

She stared at him. All-powerful muscle and sexiness leaning against her counter, and she wanted to slap him. Not because of the answer he gave her. No, it was because he dared to be so damn hot and cause her desire to flare. There was also something else about him. She narrowed her gaze and studied him, and then dawning hit.

"Holy shit, you're entering your Kamirth." She did the quick math in her head. How could she forget the mating lust a male dragon entered every fifty years?

"What of it?"

Well, at least it explained his mood, which was a tad on the ugly side. Connor had always been easygoing and never quick to anger, at least not that she'd ever seen. "Even I paid attention to the teachings. I understand what happens when a male dragon enters that stage and left to his own devices for too long. Do you plan to be home in time to take care of this?" She also remembered how she had tended to his needs herself when she'd become old enough. Heat rose up her neck and to her cheeks.

His brown gaze studied her, seemed to penetrate her soul. "I have no idea how long I'll be here. The job's done when it's done, and I certainly can handle a little sexual tension."

She couldn't help notice the punctuation he put on the word *sexual*. Was he possibly referring to their relationship? Had he been unhappy with her? Had there been anyone since she'd left? Part of her was happy to think he might have stayed celibate, but he was all male. It would be unlikely he'd wait for her to return.

"Why are you being such an ass?" She pulled out a chair, realizing it was a stupid question but waited for his answer anyway.

"You left me with a note. What the fuck do you expect from me?" He pushed off the counter and moved in closer. A predator stalking its prey. "You didn't even have the decency to talk to me face-to-face. Tell me what it was I did wrong so we could work it out." He shook his head. "You seemed happy. What the hell happened?"

She wanted to tell him. Wanted to blurt out every little word, but what good would it do? It would only serve to open the well of pain she'd capped and buried deep. Yeah, call her gutless, but she wasn't about to tell him the real reason she fled. That she couldn't take the chance he would follow the rules of the elders and banish her if she was unable to give him children. That she wished she'd been born anything but a halfling. Their society left her kind feeling worthless. She was half dragon, yet she was nothing.

"I realized I didn't love you," she lied, and the pain reflected in his eyes, before he quickly regained his composure, cut straight through her.

"You were betrothed to me as a child. We don't choose our partners for love and you know that."

His words stung the opening wounds and proved she'd been right in leaving. He was correct, though. She'd been raised knowing the reasons behind the rules, even if she thought them stupid and barbaric, and they left her feeling helpless. The dragon species had been on the decline, and fertile females were like gold to them. Still, that didn't mean those who weren't should be cast out and forced to live without their families. Was she wrong in her thinking? She remembered the look of hurt in her father's eyes when she'd told her parents how she felt and was packing to leave. They'd stood by her but had tried to convince her she should talk to Connor. She'd refused, knowing he would have changed her mind.

"I'm fully aware of the rules and they suck. They're stupid and belong in the dark ages." She crossed her arms. "Find a new female."

He cocked a brow. "Do you desire that Derrick?"

She stood and moved further away from him. Across the kitchen wasn't far enough. "None of your business." This wasn't going as she had planned. Before she knew what was happening, he had her pinned against the counter. His mouth on hers. Crushing her lips and demanding she submit. Her will gave way and she opened. Hints of dark chocolate and spice danced across her tongue. He tasted as she remembered.

Damn him for making her remember.

She pushed on his chest, and finally he broke the kiss with a nip to her bottom lip. However, he still had a strong arm firmly planted on either side of her, and she couldn't move away from his hard body or the erection that pressed into her belly.

"You want Derrick?"

Her temper flared. "So what if I do!" *Do I? Or am I just trying to hurt Connor?* Why the hell did either man have to come into the picture and confuse her further?

"Fine, then take him but in the end you are mine. You will always be mine."

She managed to hide her shock but before she could respond,

Kate bounced through the door. "Oh. Sorry Jenna, I didn't know you had company. I'd heard that you had a tough night and wanted to come and check on you."

"You're not interrupting, Kate. This is Connor, and he was just leaving." Jenna managed to slip around him and head toward the door to try and make her point. She was tired, unable to think and really needed him to leave. Thankfully, he got the hint because he moved across the kitchen and stopped in front of her.

He dipped his head to her ear. "This conversation isn't done." Then he nipped her lobe before he disappeared into the darkness. She shut the door, slumping against it.

Kate raised a brow. "So, who was that perfect male specimen you've obviously been hiding?"

Jenna sighed. "It's a long story, and I really need some sleep."

"Get some rest, but later you spill."

7

Connor stormed to his truck, cursing the entire way. He was surprised his fury didn't ignite the nearby vegetation; he was so pissed. He climbed into his vehicle and slammed the door.

"What a fucking idiot!" He dropped his forehead to the steering wheel. "I just handed her off to another man." He hadn't meant to utter the words, but he'd been pissed and desperate to give her anything that would make her happy. The thought of Derrick, or any other man with their hands caressing her naked body, was like a stack of dynamite under his emotions. It threatened to explode, and his dragon would come out with it ready to battle. The urge to shift and claim the woman who belonged to him caused him to clamp his jaw so tight it throbbed.

He loved her. All he wanted was her happiness, which apparently wasn't going to come from him. Turning over the engine, he shoved the truck into reverse and backed into the turn-around. Within seconds, he was heading down the long drive. When his phone rang, hope leapt into his heart. Maybe Jenna had changed her mind. After all, he could swear she softened into him when he'd kissed her.

He looked at the display, and his hope was quickly dashed. It was the detective. He hit the button to accept the call over the truck's speakers.

"Connor here. You got something for me?"

"Maggie Smith. She owned a small coffee shop in town. Her file says she was born in New York state and recently celebrated her thirtieth birthday."

Connor turned back onto the main road. "Nothing unusual about her. Did she have a boyfriend?"

"None anyone knew about. However, it took some deep digging since she did a good job of hiding her past..."

The detective had Connor's full attention. "And?"

"I hope you're sitting. Her real name is Sarah Dunne, she wasn't born in New York, and you can add a few zeros to her age. She was a halfling."

Connor slammed on the brakes, his truck screeching to a halt. "What did you say?"

"I thought that would grab your attention. Seems she was trying real hard to hide her past. I'll email you her file."

Scratching the scruff on his face, he mumbled, "Yeah, do that." He stomped on the gas and headed toward his hotel. This case had just taken a twist he didn't like. Not one fucking bit. The name Sarah Dunne rang a bell, and he prayed to his ancestors he was wrong. Jenna had a cousin Sarah that had been cast out by her mate and the elders when she proved infertile. Jenna had been a teen at the time, but he remembered how strongly it had affected her.

He ran his fingers through his hair as he almost blew a red light. "Son of a bitch." He suddenly had a thought. Was it possible Jenna feared the same fate? Connor always thought the rules were stupid and agreed with her assessment they belonged in the dark ages. Never once had it occurred to him she would be insecure about her place in his life. Then again, how would she know he had never planned to follow the elders and their cruel ways.

Somehow, he managed to reach his hotel without incident. He grabbed his bag and headed across the parking lot for the lobby. It was going to be a long night. He would take a look at the file Ethan sent him, and do a little digging of his own, to make sure this was the same Sarah Dunne who was related to Jenna. If Sarah did indeed turn out to be her cousin, then he would have to break the news to her. Not something he looked forward to.

Jenna had crawled into bed at least half an hour ago, but she lay there wide-awake. Her body exhausted and her mind unable to focus, she wanted so badly for sleep to take over. Seemed that wasn't going to happen. Instead, Connor filled her thoughts. His lips on hers, his hard body pressing her into the counter. She wished she could burn the memory from her mind.

She rolled over and punched the pillow. "Damn you dragon!" Anger, desire, and sadness wrestled with each other for top billing on her emotional roller coaster. Maybe if she lay there long enough and stared at the wall, sleep would finally take over. Thankfully, she wasn't due to report into the station for another day.

Time ticked, yet the sandman never came. Finally, around five o'clock, she gave up. Crawling out of bed and heading for the kitchen, she spotted Kate making coffee.

"I didn't expect to see you up for hours yet."

Jenna stifled a yawn and pulled out a chair at the table. "I can't sleep. I hope that's strong coffee you're brewing."

"Yep. Should be done shortly." Kate opened a cabinet and pulled out two mugs before she reached into the refrigerator and grabbed a bottle of creamer. "Well I couldn't sleep either, so this is a perfect time for you to fill me in on Mr. Delicious."

Jenna groaned. She didn't want to talk about Connor. He was the whole reason she was in such a twist, but maybe it would be good therapy for her. Her friend might even offer some sound advice on what to do. Kate placed a steaming cup of coffee on the table in front of her. Jenna grabbed the mug and took a sip. "Where to start?"

"The beginning's always good."

"Connor is my fiancé." Might as well get that out in the open first thing. Poor Kate choked on her coffee. "Sorry, I didn't mean to shock you."

"No, that's quite all right." Kate waved her hand. "Please continue, you have my undivided attention."

"It's true, I was betrothed to him as a child. When I was old enough, we dated…" She took another sip of coffee and contemplated for a moment before continuing. "For a few hundred years. He proposed, and I realized it wouldn't work so I ran."

Kate blinked. "Forgive me. I'm still stuck at the "few hundred years" part. Why did it take you so long to realize it wouldn't work?"

Heat raced across her cheeks. "It's rather complicated, but in our society, being a halfling is not a good thing."

A frown creased Kate's forehead but she remained silent.

"When a male dragon mates with a human, the female becomes a halfling. She takes power from her mate and as long as he lives, she does too. These unions can produce one of five types of children." Jenna sipped more caffeine before continuing. "Stay with me, this gets complicated. A male is always born a full-blooded shifter, gaining all of his father's power and abilities."

Kate nodded. "No halfling males. Got it."

"Females can be born full-blooded shifters too, though they are more rare. Or, they can be full-blooded humans and therefore can mate with a dragon. The humans are given the choice to stay in our world or integrate into human society." She stopped to eye Kate.

"I'm still with ya."

"Commonly though, the girls born are halflings. Of those, eighty percent will bear children, and the couple stands a seventy-five percent chance of having a girl who is pure shifter. This is why halflings are so important. Not even shifter-human matings have those kinds of odds."

Kate shook her head. "What about the other twenty percent?"

Jenna drew in a breath. "They will not be able to have children with a shifter. Unfortunately, this isn't discovered until after a couple are mated, and her body refuses to fertilize an egg. At that point, the male is within his right, and encouraged by the elders, to banish his mate and take another. These women are expected to leave our society forever."

"Oh. My. Fucking. God!" Kate snapped her jaw shut. "That's... That's wrong in so many ways."

"Yeah. These women are considered useless and tossed from our world." Jenna stared into her mug and studied the caramel-colored liquid as if she would be tested on it later. "I loved Connor. Still do, and it's because of that I ran." She met Kate's gaze. "I couldn't stomach the thought of him doing that to me." She felt the tears well up. "Now he's here and outright told me I could sleep with Derrick, but he refuses to let me go. I'm weak when it comes to him, and now I feel like I need to run again."

The tears came.

Kate jumped from her seat and rushed over. Kneeling down, she threw her arms around Jenna. "Sweetie, what can I do to help? Can you go to these elders and talk to them? I mean, there is an eighty-percent chance you'll have lots of dragon babies. Right?"

She shook her head. "It won't do any good. They are set in their ways, and until they are replaced with younger, more liberal members, nothing will change. Besides, I couldn't bear starting our life together only to have it ripped away."

Kate leaned back and sighed. The look in her eyes said she understood. "Is that why Connor is here? Did he come to take you back?"

"No," she let out a choked laugh. "He was called in on an arson job." Jenna shook her head and wiped her palm across her cheek. "He says he wants me, but he never looked for me. He's an excellent tracker, so it's not as if I could hide from him. Then he gives me that soul-searing kiss and tells me to sleep with Derrick? It just doesn't make any sense."

Kate stood up and pulled out a chair next to Jenna. "Yeah, that doesn't make much sense. Then again, I don't really understand your culture. Is it possible to talk to him? I mean, have you ever tried to tell him how you feel? Maybe he doesn't have the same views as the elders." She patted Jenna's hand. "If he loves you, I would think—"

"That's just it. He doesn't love me. Maybe if he did, I might convince him to leave and start a new life away from the clan."

"You mean in all the years you were together, he never told you he loved you?"

"Not once." The words burned her throat like a bitter pill.

"Jenna? Did you ever tell *him* that you loved him?"

"I... No." She chewed her lip, feeling even more guilty and confused.

Kate shook her head. "I'm no expert, but I think you should really talk to him. You two need to hash things out, and he needs to know how you feel about him." She gripped Jenna's hand. "He needs to understand what your society has done. How they have brainwashed you and probably many other women into thinking they were worthless." She leaned back. "I love you like a sister, and you know I'll do whatever I can to help you. If you need somewhere to hide out, I have some friends that live out West. You just say the word and I'll contact them, but please think about what I've said."

Jenna forced a smile. "Thanks."

8

Connor slipped into his room, set his laptop bag on the bed, and shoved his suitcase to the side. Going to the mini fridge, he pulled open the door to check out what was inside. Two bottles of water, various small bottles of liquor, a couple of candy bars, and a bottle of wine. "What? No fucking beer?" he growled under his breath and grabbed a bottle of water. Rather than drinking it, he held it to his forehead.

"Is this what human females feel like when they're having a hot flash?" He swore he was going to spontaneously combust. If he'd been a smart man, he would've told his commander he was coming into his Kamirth, and maybe a replacement would have been sent to Dallas instead. But Connor was a stubborn man, so here he was in a hotel room, feeling like he was going to set the furniture on fire. His dick was hard as steel. He pushed all thoughts of sex to the back of his mind. He'd take care of it later. Right now, he had an investigation and a job to do.

He pulled his laptop from the bag, walked to the small sofa, and plopped down. Flipping open the lid on his Mac, he looked to see if his friend Jake was online. The shifter loved to play those stupid poker games, so it was common for him to stay up until ungodly hours of the morning.

As luck would have it, Jake was online. He sent his friend a quick message through instant chat.

Connor: Hey, I need a favor and it's official business.

Jake: Sure thing.

Connor switched over to the private website his commander had set up. There they could have a conversation without fear of being hacked. Even the shifters had geeks who kept their technology locked down so tight no one would ever break through.

Jake's avatar, the Grim Reaper, popped into the chat room. The kid had a warped sense of humor that was for sure.

Jake: What's up?

Connor: I need you to dig up info on a Sarah Dunne. I believe she was a halfling, who was thrown out by Silo McGregor.

Jake: Why we looking for this girl?

Connor: She was just murdered.

Jake: Shit, good reason.

Connor: Exactly. Get on it. Make sure you send any info you find no matter how small.

Jake: Will do.

Connor set his laptop next to him and pushed off the couch. He was in need of a shower. Well, maybe not so much a shower as other things. Thoughts of Jenna raced through his mind again, and his cock answered with a twitch that caused him further irritation. Pulling his shirt over his head, he toed off his boots then fumbled with the button on his jeans. Finally, he managed to shove them off and headed for the bathroom. Standing in front of the tinted glass door, he debated on hot or cold and decided somewhere in the middle, as he reached in and turned on the water. Once inside, he realized he forgot to grab the bar of soap and shampoo off the counter. Cursing, he stepped back out, dripping water everywhere, and grabbed the items he needed.

He quickly lathered, trying to scrub the scent of Jenna off of him. Yet, he could still smell her. With a sigh, he tossed the soap into the dish and rinsed. Next, he popped open the bottle of shampoo and poured a big dollop in his hand before he stuck his head under the water. Once done, he did another quick rinse. He glanced down and stared at his cock, which jutted out in front of him. He was sick to death of having to take care of *things* himself, but what had he expected? After all, he'd practically given his fiancée to another man or at least had given her permission to go fuck one.

He banged his head against the tile wall. "Stupid. Stupid. Stupid." What he should have done was put the woman over his knee as punishment for running away.

His cock apparently loved the idea because it responded with an aching throb. In order to keep a semi-clear head, he would have to take care of business. He reached for his dick, gave it a slow stroke, and closed his eyes. Jenna once again appeared in his vision.

He missed her. But until tonight when he'd seen her, stared into those beautiful eyes and kissed her soft lips, he hadn't realized how much. Maybe it was because he'd thrown himself into his work. Some would say, even gone so far as to become reckless. Perhaps they were right. All he'd wanted to do was try and cover up her memory.

He stroked from root to head, giving the tip a slight squeeze. He let out a moan, recalling the last time he'd buried his cock deep inside her. They'd always been great together, and she'd certainly been able to handle him the last time he entered his Kamirth. What he wouldn't give to be with her right now. To have her lips wrapped around his shaft instead of his damn hand doing the deed. Keeping the vision in his head, he stroked faster. Striving to forget where he was and simply submerse himself in his little fantasy.

Moments later, he found release. Disgusted with himself and his entire species, he finished rinsing off and stepped from the shower. Grabbing a nearby towel, he quickly dried then wrapped it around his waist and exited the bathroom. Anxious to get his mind back on his work, instead of the woman who wanted nothing to do with him, he went straight for his laptop. Waking it from its slumber, he searched for anything from Jake. He wasn't surprised to see a message flashing on the screen, and he quickly tapped the button to open it.

Jake: Hey, it wasn't hard to find a file on Sarah. Here's a link to all the information we have in the database.

Connor tapped the mouse pad and clicked the link. Within seconds, a file downloaded. He opened it and scanned the contents. Pretty much as he figured. Sarah was a halfling, and her mate had tossed her aside, like a bag of trash, for another woman.

Connor felt his anger stir; the dragon buried deep inside him wanted to claw its way out. It was normal to want to shift when under emotional duress, but he managed to fight the urge. He certainly wasn't in agreement with the ways of the elders, and this would be a prime example of why it was so wrong. He couldn't understand how a male could let his mate go.

Isn't that what you did?

He supposed by not going after her, he had done just that. Deep in his gut, he realized he should have followed his instinct rather than advice from others and went in search of her. It was time to make amends and win her back. He wasn't sure if he believed Jenna when she said she didn't love him.

A woman, one of their own, had been forced from their society with no family or protection from her mate, and now she was dead. Had her attacker known who and what she was? Or was she simply a victim in the wrong place at the wrong time? These were questions he meant to answer, and when he did, someone sure as hell was going to pay.

He followed the words down to the middle of the page and quickly found the names of her parents.

"Fuck." He was going to have to tell Jenna her cousin was dead. No, not dead. Murdered.

He looked over at the clock. It was now five in the morning. Maybe he could catch a few hours of sleep before he had to meet up with the detective and scout out the crime scene.

Jenna felt slightly better after talking with Kate. She told her things that were forbidden, but at this point, she didn't care. She really needed a friend, and Kate was that friend.

"Kate, I think I'm going to take a shower."

"Good idea, it'll make you feel better. Maybe when you're done, we can talk some more and come up with a plan." Kate gave her a quick squeeze before she let go and stepped back.

Jenna shuffled off to the bathroom, stopping to grab a fresh towel out of the linen closet on her way. Behind the closed door, she stripped and turned on the water. Sticking her hand under the stream to give it a test, she decided it needed to be a touch cooler so she adjusted the temperature. Slipping in under the spray, she wet her hair then allowed the water to cascade down her back. Heat and pain throbbed between her thighs. Apparently, her body still reacted to being in close proximity to her mate. Add to it he was coming into his Kamirth, and it doubled her desire.

She reached around and turned the knob toward cold. She wasn't sure if she would ever be able to get the water cold enough. It was her duty to take care of him. To sate his primal instinct and needs. Something only a dragon or halfling could do. No human woman would quench a male's thirst when he was entering this stage in his life. For a male in the Kamirth to try and mate with a human woman would prove disastrous. Could even potentially end in her death.

Jenna grabbed the shampoo and squirted some into her hand. She quickly rubbed it through her hair and scrubbed her scalp harder than she meant to. Right now, she'd do anything to try and wash away her desire. Her urge to run out of the bathroom and find Connor, no matter where he was, almost had her doing just that. Cognizant of the fact she was capable of locating him made it even more difficult to keep her feet planted firmly where they were. Only sheer determination kept her under the spray of water.

Once she finally finished rinsing her hair, she turned off the water and reached around the curtain for a towel. Mostly dry, except for the droplets that fell from her hair, she exited the shower and caught her reflection in the mirror. Dark circles still sat under her eyes. She'd not gotten enough rest after saving the baby, so she needed some protein. It would kick-start her dragon DNA and help her recover faster. She was in desperate need of a clear mind so she could decide what to do. Running away was not an option. Not again. She loved the life she'd started here. She had a nice home, a good job, and friends.

Her mother had also recently emailed her. She and her sister, Jenna's aunt, suspected Jenna's cousin Sarah was also somewhere in or near Dallas. The girl had been sent away years ago after her mate discovered she couldn't bear him any children. Another reason Jenna fled. If it happened to family, then she was likely to face the same fate.

Jenna scampered to her room and quickly dressed in a pair of shorts and a tank top. Coming out of her room, a delicious smell wafted through the hallway and made her mouth water.

"Bacon." She followed the scent to the kitchen. Kate stood over a frying pan, one hand on her hip and the other holding a pair of tongs. She looked over at Jenna.

"You need to eat, so I decided to make breakfast. Bacon and cheese omelet, how's that sound?"

Jenna came up to stand beside Kate. "Oh my God. I'm starving and in serious need of some protein." She kissed her friend on the cheek. "You are simply the best."

Kate smiled as she poured the eggs into the other skillet. "Well then grab some plates and get the table ready."

Jenna didn't need to be told twice. She grabbed plates from the cabinet and pulled open the drawer to dig out silverware. By the time she had the table set, including napkins and glasses, Kate was loading up a plate with bacon and setting it on the table.

"Orange juice?" Jenna asked, holding open the refrigerator door.

"Please."

Jenna filled two glasses and put the container back in the refrigerator. Again, her timing was perfect as Kate slid an omelet from the pan and onto Jenna's plate.

"You first," Kate said.

Jenna piled several strips of bacon on her plate, grabbed her fork, and dug into the eggs. The cheesy goodness burst across her tongue, and she moaned as she chewed then swallowed. "This is like the best ever." She shoved a piece of bacon in her mouth.

Kate rolled her eyes. "You're just hungry, that's all. I mean it's not like a gourmet meal. Just bacon and eggs." She pulled out the chair across from Jenna, sat, and dug into her own eggs. "Though I must say, I do make a pretty mean cheese omelet," she giggled.

"I'll say."

The girls remained quiet as they polished off their breakfast. When they were done, Jenna cleared the table and loaded the dishes into the dishwasher. It was then Kate finally spoke up.

"So, have you thought about what you're going to do?"

Jenna turned and leaned against the counter, facing her friend. "Yes. I realized it's time I faced Connor and told him the truth. Well, some of it anyway."

Kate looked at Jenna for the longest while before she finally responded, "What do you mean exactly by *some of it*?"

"Tell him what my fears are, but I'm not admitting my feelings for him." She looked down at her hands as she rubbed her thumb. "I can't open that wound yet. I need to keep a wall around my heart. Maybe if he understands my fears, he'll finally let me go."

Kate let out a sigh. "Oh Jenna, I understand you're afraid, but I still think it's best if you clear the air. You need to come clean and tell him everything, including how you feel. Maybe he'll surprise you."

Before Jenna could reply, there was a knock at the door. "Are you expecting company?"

"No," Kate replied and went to answer the front door. Seconds later, Derrick stepped into the kitchen.

"Hi, Jenna. I came to check on you and see how you're doing."

Jenna smiled back at him, actually happy to see him. Even more so, now that she'd decided to come clean with Connor. She also had some explaining to do about the whole fiancé thing she'd thrown at him last night.

9

Connor woke and stretched, feeling more agitated than when he'd lain down to take a quick nap. He looked at the clock; he'd only been asleep — if that's what you wanted to call it — for about an hour. He rolled out of bed and walked naked to the suitcase he still hadn't unpacked. Flipping it open, he pulled out a pair of jeans and slipped them on, leaving them unbuttoned. He dug for a T-shirt and pulled it over his head then tucked it into his pants before zipping them up.

Heading into the bathroom, he ran a comb through his hair and quickly brushed his teeth. Hopefully, he'd be able to get on the crime scene so he could do a little investigation of his own. Going back into the other room, he grabbed his black boots, pulled them on, and shoved his laptop into the bag. Snatching his phone off the nightstand, he dialed the detective as he headed out the door.

"Ethan. I need to get on the scene so I can check things out. I also have more information on the girl."

"Sure thing. They're expecting you. I'll meet you there, in say, twenty minutes?"

Connor headed for the elevator and pressed the button. "Yeah, sounds good. I'll see you there."

"I'm stopping for coffee. Can I get you anything?"

Connor entered the elevator and hit the button for the lobby. "Large with cream. And thanks." He hung up as the doors swung open to the lobby. He strode across to the exit and stepped outside. Already the August heat of Dallas was stifling. "Jesus Christ. How do these people put up with this?" His ancestors originated high in the mountains, where summers were mild and winters brutal. He'd much rather face cold, blustery winds and the snow of winter than this shit. The only reason they were firefighters was because they were damn good at it and loved it. Otherwise, in human form, fire could harm them like any other mortal.

He crossed the parking lot and pulled open the door on his truck, cursing under his breath as the steam blasted him in the face. He climbed in, started the engine, and quickly cranked the air-conditioning to high. Pulling from the lot, he made his way across town in good time and was on the crime scene before Ethan. He exited his truck and approached an officer, who stood in front of the crime scene tape.

"Sorry, this place is off-limits," the young officer stated, pulling his shoulders back. He was a good six inches shorter and far less muscular than Connor. Puffing his chest wasn't going to do him a damn bit of good.

Connor looked around, trying to see who else was there. "I'm part of the investigation team. Names Connor O'Rourke."

The kid's eyes widened. "Oh, yes, sir. I've been instructed to let you in when you show up. Go on ahead."

Connor lifted the tape and walked under it. Picking his way across the small front yard, he stepped over burned debris that had been scattered in the wind. He stopped and inhaled.

Still nothing but the stench of a smoldering fire. Maybe if he got closer, he could catch the assailant's scent.

"Good morning. I'm Arson Investigator Tim Johnson, and this is Detective Sam Patterson. You must be O'Rourke. We've been expecting you."

"I am. I was here last night, but can you fill me in on the details?" He stuck his hand out to shake the other gentlemen's hands.

"So far as we can tell, our victim Maggie Smith was bound and gagged and left here in the closet. She had a wound on the back of her head, indicating she had been struck with something," Sam stated, shaking his head. "She was also naked, though that could just be how she slept. However, the coroner is checking for sexual assault. Hopefully, we'll have more answers later as to whether or not she died from the head injury or smoke inhalation."

Connor nodded. "I detect gasoline, the same MO as our arsonist."

"You'd be correct. We have no way to know if it's the same guy." Tim ran his fingers through his short, gray hair. "This is the first time we've had a victim that was clearly murdered."

Connor stepped into the large walk-in closet. One wall was totally burned away, while the others were only covered with soot. "I would tend to disagree that this is your criminal's first murder. You had victims in the other fires, just not any who were bound and gagged and shoved into a closet." The investigator turned a little red in the face.

"True. Poor choice of words on my part." Tim moved up next to him and pointed. "She was found over here, lying on her side, hands bound behind her back. She was facing this wall over here." He indicated with a nod that her back had been to the wall that was now burned away. "Of course you probably already know all of this."

Connor stared at the floor. Blood stained the carpet where her head had obviously been, and once again, anger coiled in his stomach. How the hell was he going to tell Jenna her cousin was dead, likely raped and definitely murdered? "I do, but I appreciate the confirmation. If you don't mind, I'm going to take a look around, see what I can find."

Sam nodded. "Let us know if you need anything. We need to find this bastard and stop him."

"Agreed."

"So, you're telling me Connor is your fiancé, yet he's not?" Derrick questioned, a perplexed look on his face.

Jenna wasn't sure how she could explain it so he would understand. Hell, it was so different from what humans were used to. They had abolished arranged marriages decades ago. "Yes, that's pretty much what I'm telling you. I haven't seen him in at least a year, and I've already asked him to break our bond."

He scratched his chin and stared at her with those baby blues. "What do you mean by bond?"

"It's complicated, I know. A blood bond was formed between Connor and I when I was a baby. It means we have a connection. We sense each other's moods and can find each other no matter where we are. This initial bond tells a dragon male I belong to another. Once a couple decides to actually mate, they complete that bond. It involves sex and magic..." Her cheeks heated at the thought of Connor performing the ritual. "I can't go into detail, but the couple are then tied together. The female is given power and a longer life expectancy from her male. If not already formed, a telepathic link begins. The bond I have now with Connor can be broken, however. He just has to go to my father and say he no longer wishes me for his mate."

He shifted his weight on the couch next to her. "Jenna. You must know I like you. A lot. And if there's really nothing between you and Connor then I wonder if maybe I stand a chance? I mean of having a real date with you."

"I like you too, Derrick. I don't see any reason why we couldn't go out." Tension snapped in the air as he leaned in closer.

"Is it okay to kiss you?" he whispered.

She swallowed. Her mind said no. *You love Connor and belong to him.* Her body screamed, *yes, yes, yes!* Maybe this would be good for her. A test of sorts to see if there was something between her and Derrick.

"Yes."

Their lips were now only inches apart. Her breathing hitched when he finally brought his mouth to hers in a gentle kiss. She parted her lips, and he swiped his tongue across hers. He tasted different but not in a bad way. Smoky. Her lust stirred slightly but not as it did with Connor. *Damn him.*

Derrick pulled back and rubbed his thumb across her cheek. "My shift will be starting soon, so I have to get going. You just let me know when you're ready for that date, and I'll make it happen."

"Okay. Stay safe."

He pushed off the couch and headed for the door. "I'll call you later."

"That would be great," she replied as she walked him outside. Derrick stepped off the porch, and a truck pulled up the driveway. Jenna instantly recognized Connor, and if it were possible, her heart both flipped and sank at the same time. Derrick simply turned and gave her a questioning look, and she shrugged her shoulders. He nodded and continued on to his own truck.

"Connor, nice morning," Derrick stated as he passed.

"I hope it wasn't *too* nice," Connor growled back. In three steps, he reached Jenna on the porch. "Jenna, I have some news. Where can we talk in private?"

She sensed the turmoil inside him and worried what he had to tell her. Had he changed his mind? "We can go inside. Kate is just leaving to do some shopping, so we'll have the house to ourselves." She led him into the living room. "Can I get you something to drink?"

"I'm fine, thanks."

Kate stuck her head around the corner. "Hey, Jenna, I'm getting ready to head out. Is there something you want me to pick up?"

"I can't think of anything, but if I do I'll send you a text."

Kate nodded. "Sounds good. See you later. Hi, Connor." She gave a little wave and he nodded.

"So, what's this bad news you have to tell me?" She took a seat in the chair across from the couch, not wanting to get too close to him. All kinds of craziness ran through her mind as to the bad news, so she shut it off and just waited for him to tell her.

He cleared his throat. "You remember I told you I was here investigating some arsons?"

"Yes, of course."

"Well, last night there was an actual murder. The girl was bound, gagged, and locked in a closet then her house set on fire." Connor stared at her as if waiting to gauge her reaction.

"Oh my God, that's horrible!" Jenna couldn't imagine and prayed the girl was already dead when she was locked in that closet with a fire burning around her.

"I... Shit." He scrubbed the scruff on his chin.

"What is it, Connor?" Her body stiffened.

"I'm so sorry, love," he whispered. "The girl was your cousin Sarah."

Jenna bit her lip. Numbness took over her limbs, and she tried to comprehend the words he had just spoken. "That can't be right. There has to be a mistake." She jumped from her seat, and he was there to pull her into his arms. "You made a mistake." She lashed out and pummeled his chest, but he only squeezed her tighter.

"I can't take away your pain, but you can take your pain out on me. I'm here." He kissed her temple. "I'm here, baby."

The dam broke and she sobbed. Cried for the tragic death in her family. Screamed at the treatment of her kind by the elders. Cursed the one thing she could not deny. The man who held her was the only one she wanted. She'd been fooling herself every time she said otherwise. Relaxing into him felt right in so many ways.

"I'm really sorry, but there was no mistake. It's definitely her. She had assumed a new identity and was going by the name of Maggie Smith. I... I hate to ask, but I was hoping you might be able to help me. Tell me anything you might know about what she's been doing."

Jenna leaned back and searched his face. The sincerity she saw was genuine. "How could anybody want to hurt her like that? This has to be a horrible nightmare, and I'll wake up soon." She dropped her head to his chest and cried again. The motion of his hand rubbing her back was like a balm on an open wound.

Soothing.

He kissed the top of her head and she melted. Jenna had to come back to her senses, so she pried herself free from his comforting arms. "I don't know how I can help you, but I'll do anything I can. Promise me you will find the bastard that did this."

He rubbed his thumb across her cheek, wiping away a tear. "I will kill him myself."

Jenna knew he would, but she couldn't allow him to break the law like that. "No. Promise me you won't. As much as I would like to see dragon law upheld here, we have to follow the human rules."

A scowl formed on his face. "I will only do it because you ask it of me. I know this is difficult, but do you know of any enemies Sarah might've had? Though I assume this was someone she knew, it's possible. it was just another random arson. The perpetrator has simply gone from setting fires to committing murder."

Jenna thought for a moment. She hadn't seen her cousin since Sarah had left home, abandoned by her mate. Had she known sooner that her cousin had been in Dallas, she would've looked her up. Now she was riddled with guilt. "I feel like I don't know anything about her, she's been gone so long." She sniffed. "I've only recently told my parents where I'm living. Sarah's mom mentioned she thought Sarah might be here. Damn, how am I going to break the news to her?"

Again, his eyes filled with understanding. "Would you like me to call her?"

"No. It should come from family, but I appreciate the thought." She stared into his brown eyes and almost lost herself, until she quickly jerked free of his invisible hold. This was the worst time ever to bring up her situation with Connor; it also seemed the perfect time, and she felt comfortable in doing so.

"This brings me to something I need to talk to you about," she whispered.

He stayed by her side and took her hand in his. "Go ahead. You can tell me anything."

She closed her eyes for a moment and pulled in a long deep breath, searching for courage before she focused on his handsome face. "I feel it's only fair you understand the reason why I want you to break our bond. Why I left. What's happened with Sarah is a perfect example. I'm a halfling same as she, and I don't want what happened to her to also happen to me. You know there's a good chance in the world I cannot give you children."

He squeezed her hand. "When have you ever known me to follow the rules?"

She blinked but couldn't answer.

"I understand how you feel, and I agree with your assessment that our ways are outdated." He released her and stepped back. She missed his warmth. "I had fully resigned myself to the fact that if you indeed turned out to be barren, then we would remain childless or perhaps consider adoption. I would never break my vow to you."

She was stunned. "How come you never told me how you felt about our ways?"

"I never realized it was something that bothered you. Then when you up and left, I was devastated. I wanted to look for you. Know that I fought with myself every second to keep from dropping everything and demanding you come home."

"Why didn't you then?"

"I thought maybe if you were given some time to yourself, you'd come back. Your parents even thought it might be wise to give you some space. And I'll admit, I couldn't take you rejecting me again."

"I had no idea." She looked down at her fingers as she plopped back into the chair. "This mess between us is all my fault."

"You're not to blame. I should've been more open, told you how I felt but I was an idiot. It has to be hard on a woman in our society. After all, you're betrothed to a man when you're only an infant. You're never allowed to experience the world, be with other men, or choose for yourself the one you want to spend the rest of your life with."

He surprised her, and she realized there were far more layers to this man than she had ever known. How could she have spent all that time with him, yet missed so much? Only moments ago, she had confessed interest in another man. Now? She couldn't be more confused. She had loved Connor once. Still did, if she stopped lying to herself. But she had been an idiot and ran off like a little girl instead of facing things like an adult. Where did that leave them now?

"Things need to change in our society, or it will continue to get worse," she stated.

He steeled his features. "Then it shall start with me. I will give you back your life, Jenna. I will break the tie that has already begun between us, so you can be free to choose the life you want. Maybe we can set the example that couples should choose one another and fall in love. Not be forced into a relationship."

She pushed to her feet, feeling a little unsteady. *He doesn't love me. He so much as said so.* "I'm not sure what to say. Thank you." His promise to give her what she'd been begging for now left her confused. One minute he claimed she belonged to him and now...

There was still one more thing she had to do. Give him back his dignity. The hurt that had been reflected in his eyes when he'd confessed how he felt after she left still cut through her. "I'm sorry for leaving you with only a note. It was wrong and it was childish. I loved you, Connor. It's why I had to leave. It would have ripped my heart in two if you had turned your back on me."

His deep brown gaze bore into her. "And what about now, Jenna? Do you still love me?"

She wanted to say yes, but fear sunk its claws into her and kept her from opening that place where they had once been happy. "I-I'm not sure how I feel." *Liar!*

"Honest answer and fair enough. The choices are now yours to make. If you decide it's the fireman you want, then I wish you all the happiness."

Jenna felt like one weight had been lifted off her shoulders only to be replaced with another. Her freedom had been what she wanted, but now that it was being granted to her, it left her feeling empty. Was she crazy? Why couldn't she decide who or what she desired? Part of her wanted to explore a relationship with Derrick. After all, he was human and there was no doubt with a human male she would have a family.

With Connor, there was that nagging question, even though he had reassured her how he felt about the situation. While the two of them had enjoyed a good relationship, he had never once said he loved her. Oh sure, she'd felt adored and taken care of, but a woman needed to know the man she was going to spend the rest of her life with loved her with every fiber of his being. How she wished when she confessed moments ago, he would have told her how he felt.

I'm not playing fair. I didn't tell him I still love him. Could he be as insecure as she was? It was difficult to imagine this tall, dangerous dragon as insecure.

What the hell was she going to do?

Push all of this aside and take one step at a time. In the meantime, she had to focus on the murder of her cousin, and they had to find the killer. With renewed confidence, she lifted her chin. "The first thing we need to do is find my cousin's murderer. I'm going to help you, and I'm not taking no for an answer."

He nodded. "I appreciate the help. As soon as I can get back home, I'll seek out your father and break our bond." Jenna's father was the one who bonded them together, and therefore would have to unweave his magic. "Of course, you do realize your father could betroth you to another?"

"He won't." There was also something else, a big dark monster that lurked in the room and needed to be addressed. "Connor, you have to promise me, if your Kamirth reaches a critical point, you will let me help." The thought of him suffering ate at her, and the fact he might have to seek another was like a knife in her heart.

"Jenna?" Her name rolled off his lips in a snarl.

She held her hand up. "I know this is opening up a can of worms, so to speak, but I can't have you going around half-crazed and threatening society."

"It won't come to that."

"I still have a duty to you until our bond is severed." *And maybe I just want one last time together.*

His mouth drew into a tight line. "Maybe you should have thought of that *before* you left me."

Ouch. She deserved that, but it didn't stop the sting.

10

Connor tried to keep his eyes on the road and not stare at Jenna, who sat on the other side of the truck. His temper was in rare form.

Again.

Why the hell didn't I tell her how I felt? Because he was an idiot when it came to her. Did love make human males stupid as well? He seemed to recall Quinn doing dumb shit in the name of love. There was also the fact Derrick's scent was all over her. When he'd met the prick coming out of her house, he wanted to kill him. Slice his belly open and let his guts spill all over the ground. It's what any self-respecting dragon would do when another male threatened his territory. However, Jenna was a halfling. Even though her father was a dragon and she understood the culture, he didn't think he'd score any points by acting rash. She had to decide once and for all what, or in this case, who she wanted.

The detective called earlier and said something about being at Sarah's coffee shop. Connor had proposed the idea of bringing Jenna down to talk to him and maybe take a look around to see if she could find anything. What, he had no idea, but now they sat in silence on the drive back to town, and he felt like an awkward schoolboy.

The dragon part of him grinned at the remembrance of her promise to take care of his sexual needs should they become too "out-of-control." He was half-tempted to take her up on said offer as a means to keep her close. Remind her of what they were like together. But would that guarantee her love? He feared it would only make things worse, but damn his reserve was dwindling.

His sensible side said it would be wrong to take advantage of her. Even after their conversation, he was still unsure of where they stood. He'd made a partial confession and meant what he said about letting her go if it was really what she wanted. It didn't mean he wouldn't try and wheedle his way back into her life. She may not know how she felt, but he sure as hell did. Should he have told her he loved her? It was times such as these he really missed his own mother.

"Why are you growling?"

Connor was jerked back by Jenna's sweet voice. "What?"

Her gaze was pinned on him. "You were growling."

"Oh. Uh, I was thinking about finding the asshole setting these fires." It wasn't a total lie. Jenna was struck hard by the loss of her cousin and that pissed him off. No one was allowed to hurt the woman he loved like that and get away with it.

She gave him a slight smile. "It was kind of you to offer to drive me. I'm not sure I was really up to it myself."

"It's the least I can do. Anything else you need, just let me know. I'm here for you."

"Thanks. That means a lot to me."

Connor maneuvered the truck into a parking space behind the coffee shop. He figured it was better to go in the back rather than the front. He hurried around and opened the door for Jenna, offering his hand to help her out of the truck. He escorted her to the back door and pulled it open, holding it until she stepped through before he came up behind her. He spotted Ethan right away and angled her in his direction.

"Detective, this is Jenna, Sarah's cousin." Connor took a step back so the two could exchange handshakes.

"Miss Dunne, I'm so sorry for your loss. Believe me, we're doing everything we can to find the person or persons responsible for her death. Of course, anything you can offer would be most helpful," the detective replied.

Jenna offered a forced smile. "Thank you, Detective. I don't know what I can offer since I haven't seen my cousin in several years. As a matter of fact, I hadn't even realized she was in Dallas. However, I'll do everything I can to help find whoever did this."

"I'll be perfectly honest, we don't have a lot to go on right now. We thought maybe if we came down here, and looked through some of her records, we might find something. So far it's only been the usual stuff." Ethan took a couple steps away and grabbed a box. "We did find these photographs, which seems strange to keep something like this here rather than at home. Would you mind looking at them and see if you recognize anyone?"

"Of course."

The detective set the box on a nearby table and opened it up. Connor escorted Jenna to a chair and pulled it out so she could have a seat. She reached into the box and retrieved a worn, leather photo album. She carefully flipped open the cover to the first page, and Connor could tell she was fighting the tears.

"I recognize that photo," Connor spoke softly. "It's you and Sarah."

She nodded. "Yes. If I remember correctly, I was about ten in this picture."

She flipped to the next page. "This is a picture of Sarah and her parents. I think this was right before her wedding. Her family had taken her on a trip to Hawaii." She continued to flip through the album; photos from various family gatherings were pasted to the pages. When she got about halfway through, her body went stiff. Connor saw exactly what the problem was.

It was Sarah's wedding picture.

The detective arched a brow. "Would that have been her husband?"

Connor spoke up before Jenna had a chance. "Yes."

Ethan scratched at his chin. "So what happened? How long ago did they get a divorce?"

Jenna let out a laugh filled with bitterness. "In our world, there's no such thing as divorce. You see detective, my cousin was unable to have children. Therefore, her husband—as you call him—tossed her out. Her family and her people turned their back on her."

Ethan looked shocked and lifted his head to search Connor's face. Connor gave a nod. "What she says is true. Our ways are a little barbaric."

"I see." The detective reached into his shirt pocket for a pad and pen and began scratching. "I'd like to talk to this gentleman. Ask him some questions."

"I'm sure I can arrange that," Connor stated as he walked away. He moved around the front of the coffee shop, sniffing to see if he could recognize any of the scents. He picked up coffee and a few bakery items, but there were so many human signatures from customers who'd come in and out, he couldn't really place his finger on any one scent. Nothing matched the fire scene, so he was fairly positive the perpetrator hadn't been here. At least, not up front as a customer. Maybe he'd find something in the back.

As he started to make his way to where he assumed Sarah's office would be, along with the storage area, there was a commotion in the front. He heard unfamiliar footsteps before the human even spoke.

"I must speak to whoever's in charge here," a determined voice bounced off the ceramic tiles.

Connor headed toward the voice, his senses and body on full alert. He would protect Jenna at all costs. "Who the hell are you?" He towered over the much shorter balding man, who appeared to be in his late fifties and wore an expensive gray suit.

The gentleman stuck out his hand. "My name is Mr. Sampson. I am, I mean I was Miss Dunne's attorney." He moved his black briefcase from one hand to the other and shook his head, looking down at the floor before his gaze came back to meet Connor's. "Such a terrible tragedy."

Ethan rounded up next to Connor and stuck his hand out. "Mr.

Sampson, I'm Ethan Collins, the detective in charge here. I understand someone from the department found your card in the victim's belongings and called you. We're hoping you might be able to provide some information regarding Sarah Dunne."

The man pulled his shoulders back. "Of course, I'll certainly do whatever I can to help." He stepped to a nearby table and laid his briefcase down. Clicking open the snaps, he opened the case and pulled out a manila folder. Clearing his throat, he asked, "I do wonder though, if you might also be able to assist me? Miss Dunne did name a sole heir. Of course, there isn't much left of her home, but the shop and the money she had in her accounts were left to a family member."

Connor and Ethan glanced at each other before the detective spoke. "And who did she name as her heir?"

The man flipped open the folder and ran his finger down the page. "A cousin by the name of Jenna Dunne."

Jenna jumped from her seat. "I'm Jenna. Jenna Dunne." She moved next to Connor and brushed against him. He wrapped his arm around her shoulders and pulled her close, sensing she needed his strength.

"I haven't seen my cousin in years. I don't understand why she would leave her belongings to me."

Mr. Sampson looked up from his folder. "It's not for me to question who a client wishes to leave their estate to, only to follow through with those wishes. I'll need you to come down to my office and sign the papers. Once that's done, this place is yours and you can do with it whatever you wish, along with the hundred thousand she had in her accounts."

Jenna slapped her hand over her mouth. "I—I don't know what to say."

———

Jenna was stunned, and she leaned into the warmth and protection of Connor. So much had happened in the last forty-eight hours, and she was having a hard time processing it all. It was the detective who spoke up and broke the silence in the room.

"I'm curious, Mr. Sampson, how signing a few papers can transfer an estate so quickly? These things usually take some time." His right brow arched high. "I'm also curious on how you know the victim's legal name."

The attorney stuffed his folder back into his case and closed it. "Miss Dunne had wanted to remain anonymous here in Dallas. However, it would be difficult to own and operate a business, not to mention having a legal and binding trust, without using one's legal name. I was fully aware of Miss Dunne's background and why she wished to go by the name of Maggie Smith. I assure you, that all of this is legally binding under the Dragon Nation laws."

He looked at Jenna. "Your cousin wanted to make sure you would inherit this place along with all her assets. She knew the dragon laws would be upheld. Whenever you're ready..." He held out his business card. "Come to my office and I'll make sure everything is arranged. I'm so very sorry for your loss."

Jenna reached for the card and stared at the glossy print. "Thank you, Mr. Sampson. I'll be in touch."

The man nodded and headed out the front door that he had come in.

"Well, Miss Dunne, I'd like you to come to the station for questioning," Ethan stated.

Panic crawled up Jenna's spine. "Why do you need to see me at the station?"

"Yeah, why?" Connor stood rigid next to her, his grip on her shoulders tightening.

The detective shifted his weight in a nervous gesture. "I'm sorry, Miss Dunne. We have to clear you as a suspect in this case."

Jenna tried to suck in a breath, but her lungs refused to cooperate.

She looked down and realized her hands were shaking, and Connor squeezed her tighter. "How can I be a suspect?"

"Detective, you've just crossed the line," Connor hissed. "Besides, you know damn good and well where Jenna was when that fire started."

Ethan gathered his things. "Yes, I know she was working, and I realize she has witnesses to verify that. However, that doesn't mean she couldn't have had somebody else do the job. It's just routine questioning."

Jenna thought Connor was going to come unglued. Perhaps even shift right there in the very room where they all stood. His anger rolled off him and bounced against the walls like a wild ping-pong ball. She had to act before he lost control and did something he'd later regret. Like kill the detective.

"Fine. I'll come to the station and answer your stupid questions." She looked at Connor and placed her palm on his chest. "Look at me. It's simply a formality, and I have nothing to hide."

His gaze snapped to hers. His eyes were full of fire as he fought to control his emotions. "You will not go without an attorney." When she started to protest, he held up his hand. "I will not budge on this matter. And I will not argue."

She gave a nod of acknowledgment, realizing they were all better off if she agreed to his terms. Besides, it certainly couldn't hurt, just in case things did get out of hand. She had absolutely nothing to hide, but she'd watched enough of those crazy TV shows to worry.

"I'll call the council right now. We have people in Dallas." Connor stepped away to make a call. The council was the organization that upheld dragon law. Already she felt better knowing a member would be on her side.

11

Rage swept over Connor like a tsunami. To think Jenna would even consider doing something to harm another living soul was preposterous. The woman wouldn't kill a bug, let alone her own family. He couldn't even wrap his mind around the idea. His body still threatened to shift as he punched the contact on his phone labeled Council.

It rang twice before a female answered. "Dragon District Council, how may I direct your call?"

"I need the Dallas branch. Please."

"One moment."

The line switched to classical music before a man picked up. "Patrick O'Donnell here. How can I help you?" Connor detected a hint of the old world in the man's voice. It comforted him.

"Patrick. Connor O'Rourke here. I need legal help for my mate. We're here in Dallas."

"Where can we meet?"

Connor rattled off the hotel where he was staying, and the two made arrangements to meet later. "Thanks, I appreciate it." He ended the call.

Detective Collins stood with arms crossed. "Seems you forgot to mention you two were an item."

"We're not," Jenna responded.

Connor grabbed her arm and ushered her toward the door. "Until things are ended, you still belong to me," he snapped. How he managed to keep his cool was a secret even he didn't understand. His Kamirth was closing in on him and making his mood fouler by the minute. His dragon wanted to free itself, and it wanted to claim Jenna. Rip her clothes off and take her here on a table. Or maybe the counter. Perhaps both. He'd kill anyone who dared watch.

He scrubbed a hand over his face. *I need to get my shit together.* "We have an appointment with an attorney later. I promise, we'll have Jenna at the station tomorrow." Thankfully, his phone chirped and he pulled it from his pocket to read the text.

Jake: You need to call me as soon as possible. Mega important!!!

Connor knew it was big for him to get a message like that. He hit the green call button.

"What the hell's up?" he asked the second Jake answered.

"We just received word of two more deaths. Halflings, bound and tossed in a closet and burned."

"Son of a bitch! Where?" Both Jenna and Ethan gave Connor a questioning look.

"One happened a week ago out in California, and the other was two weeks before that. New York. Seems it took authorities that long to get in touch with us."

"Send me all the details."

"Already done," Jake replied.

Connor ended the call and focused his gaze on the detective. "Jenna is no longer a suspect. Two more of our people were murdered in California and New York. Same MO. They're sending me the details."

Jenna gasped, her hand over her mouth.

"Well this does indeed change things, but I'd still like to officially clear Ms. Dunne. I'd like to see those files as well," Ethan replied.

Connor gave a quick nod before he turned to Jenna. "You shouldn't be alone."

"I have a shift at the station tomorrow."

"Fine, but you're not going home." He led her outside, his senses on full alert as he opened the door to his truck and helped her climb in. Once he slid into the driver seat, she spoke.

"Do you really think it's necessary? I mean I'm not in any danger."

He pinned his gaze on her. "I'm sure the others felt the same."

Her anger flared. "You can't hold me hostage. I have a life, and I don't belong to you. You promised to let me go."

He teetered on a knife's edge. "The game has changed. You're mine and that's final." He hadn't meant to shout, and the look in her eyes said she was about to go ballistic on his ass. He'd fucked up yet again. Raking his fingers through his hair, he tried to approach things from a different angle. "Damn it woman, I love you, and you can't expect me to sit by and watch another man take you." He held up his hand to silence her. "I know what I fucking said about Derrick, and I was wrong."

The fire in her hazel gaze dimmed slightly. "Then why did you tell me––"

"I'm a fucking idiot. I thought if I allowed you some freedom"––he swallowed––"you might come back to me." His grip on the steering wheel tightened until his knuckles turned white, as he waited for some kind of response from her.

"The turmoil rolling off of you is almost as suffocating as the heat outside. How close are you, exactly, to your Kamirth?" She folded her arms and continued to stare at him. He'd just confessed his feelings and she was still pissed?

He felt his lip curl into a snarl and his fangs began to extend. "I'm fine."

"Hmmm. You lie like shit too. Apparently, you've forgotten I can read you like a book. Need I remind you, we've been down this road before?" When he finally dared glance over at her, both of her brows were raised giving him a questioning look.

How the hell was he supposed to answer her? She was right

though, and there was no way he could lie to her. "I can get through this."

This time, lines of worry furrowed across her forehead. "Are you sure? Cause from where I'm sitting, you look like you're about to explode. Do you have any idea how close you were to shifting in there? If I may be so blunt, when was the last time you got laid?"

Shit, did he dare tell her? He looked away, unable to meet her gaze. "Not since you." He hoped like hell she didn't offer to share with him the last time she'd had a man between her thighs. Because seriously, he was on the edge. It would take just one little thing to push him over. Right now, he had no common sense left.

"Oh. I see."

He started his truck. "Don't sound so damn disappointed." He shoved the gearshift into reverse and backed out of his parking spot. "I don't mean to be so grouchy and snap at you. It's just... It's hard to be around you right now. Your scent alone makes me feel like a damn, drooling dog." He pulled out onto the street, realizing he wasn't even sure where the hell he was headed. *Right, the hotel.* How was he going to be in the same room as her? Maybe he could request an upgrade to a suite.

"I'm not disappointed. Surprised maybe but not disappointed. You're a handsome man, Connor, and any woman would be happy to have you. I..." She appeared uncomfortable with the conversation and shifted in her seat. "Look, I promised to help you through this so you wouldn't take off anybody's head. I haven't been with a man since we were together." She let out a sigh. "What can it hurt for us to let off a little steam? It might even clear your head so you can continue with this investigation."

He knew he should say no and drive her ass — as fine as it was — back to her place. Being with her was only going to make matters worse for him, but the head between his legs was busy shouting out "take her up on her offer!" There was also the fear for her safety, and she'd been ready to say something important. He got the feeling she was glad he'd not been with anyone since her. Damn, maybe there was still a chance for the two of them.

He loved her. She'd wanted to say the words back but they got stuck. Instead, she offered to have sex with him. There was a tinge of guilt about Derrick. She had sort of led him on earlier, and now things had changed. Hadn't they? Connor loved her, and if he could forgive her, maybe they could start over.

She swallowed, looked over at him, and watched his jaw tick. "Unless of course you have other plans."

"None that can't be changed," he responded.

They pulled up to a red light, and he finally met her stare. "Are you positive? Because teasing me right now would be the worst idea you've ever had."

Was she? Her body sure as hell was. Her mind? Maybe not as willing, but it would certainly follow along. Things were crazy right now, and a little bit of companionship might be exactly what they both needed. Even so, she knew it was what he needed. He was closer to his Kamirth than he was willing to admit, and soon he would be a danger to everyone.

"Positive." She made sure to add confidence to her reply or he might back out.

The light changed and traffic ahead of them began to move. Connor nodded. "Fine. I'm not going to ask again."

Twenty minutes later, they pulled into the hotel parking lot. Connor hardly had the truck in park and turned off before he was at her door and helping her out. He whisked her across the lot and into the lobby, where the cool air caressed her hot skin. Just the thought of what they were about to do sent a shiver down her spine and heat to her core.

This is only about the sex. We both need a release. Later we can figure out where our relationship stands.

With his hand at the small of her back, he escorted her into an empty elevator and pressed the button. The doors closed, leaving them alone. Before she could exhale, he had her arms pinned over her head and her back against the wall. His mouth slammed hard over hers, and his magic slid across her skin like a silk scarf.

There was no way the dragon in him could wait another minute. It needed to be satisfied and she could only surrender. Allow him total control of her body. This was where most human females got into trouble. Anything other than compliance would cause the dragon to use any means to make them submit. She understood the species and knew Connor no longer had control.

They would not leave this elevator until the beast was sated.

Sparks snapped along the panel, and the elevator stopped abruptly. The lights dimmed. A dragon's magic was unstoppable when they entered sexual lust, and apparently, Connor's had just played havoc with the circuitry.

His free hand slid up the back of her thigh and under her shorts. Cupping her ass in a firm grip, he spoke against her lips. "I need."

Dear god, so did she. The thought of him taking her here sent throbbing heat to her sex. "Yes."

He released her and took a step back. His brown eyes shifted between hazel and green. He was fighting to stay in control. "I shouldn't do this, not here." His voice was ruff and low, and she knew he struggled.

Without hesitation, she shoved her shorts and panties down her thighs and stepped out of them. Next, she pulled her top off and freed her breasts. "Yours." She dropped her gaze to the floor and stared at his boots. The sound of his zipper being lowered met her ears.

12

Connor pulled the belt free from his jeans and lowered the zipper, thankful he went commando. "Hold out your hands."

She did as he instructed, and he looped the belt around her wrists, pulling it tight. "On your knees and suck my cock." Again, she obeyed. The woman took his breath away. Her full breasts and rounded hips were made for fucking, and he hated himself in this moment. Hated what he was and how he would take her. Thankfully, she never tempted fate, knowing a male in his lust also had a need to be in total control and expected compliance. Even so much as eye contact could send the beast into a fit.

He dropped his pants enough to free his cock. The tip glistened with anticipation, and he could scarcely believe he was going to have her again. God, he'd missed her. She wrapped her lips around the tip of his shaft and sucked.

"Fuck." He groaned, finally had her where he'd imagined her earlier. It was no longer a dream, and he wasn't jerking off. It didn't get any more real.

She took his entire length, working her mouth up and down his shaft. He fisted her hair and rocked his hips. He inhaled. Her musky scent said she was ready. If he kept up this pace, he'd soon explode, and he wanted to be inside her when he did that.

"Enough. On your feet and face the wall," he commanded and she readily obeyed. "Bend over." She fell into position.

He slid up behind her and ran his hands down her back. A quick slap across her ass turned the cheek a nice pink. She didn't flinch or cry out, but her breathing increased. He fisted his throbbing member and parted her folds with the tip while kicking her legs apart. She let out a soft moan, and he thrust, entering her until her sex wrapped around him like a velvet glove. He bent, his lips next to her ear.

"I promise to make it up to you." Claws extended from his fingertips, sinking into the flesh of her hips and thick fangs elongated from the top and bottom of his mouth. His magic chilled the air around them until he could see every breath he exhaled.

Perfect. He sunk his claws deeper until Jenna's blood trickled down her legs and the coppery scent filled his nostrils. He moved and began a pounding thrust, eliciting a moan from her. Wings emerged from his back as he went into a partial shift.

"So hot and wet," he growled, pistoning faster. He fought the urge to finish their bond. Make her completely his. It would only take a few uttered words, a little magic, and a bite to her shoulder and she would be bound to him. She'd also hate him, and he couldn't live with that.

His balls pulled tight, and the release he desperately needed worked its way up his shaft. *Too soon.* He wanted to bask in the closeness he shared with Jenna, but the beast in him wanted to spill his seed. Later, he'd have to find a way to take things slower. With one last thrust, the fog around his brain lifted and his muscles tightened with ejaculation. With the last spasm, the chill faded in the elevator and he pulled free.

"Shit." He rubbed her hips as she straightened. Already, bruising marred her perfect skin along with the bloody wounds. "Let me heal you." He reached around and freed her wrists, rubbing them.

Jenna looked over her shoulder at him and smiled, giving a nod of approval. Damn, he loved this woman. He laved his tongue over her right hip, allowing his saliva to close the wound and ease the pain. By the time he began working on the other side, her skin was unmarred. Not a trace of what he'd done. He placed his palm on her waist and turned her to face him.

"You okay?"

"Yes."

He grabbed her panties and helped her slip them on. Next her shorts, then he handed her the top that was across the floor. "I'm sorry," he whispered, before zipping up his pants and flaring out magic to restart the elevator.

Sorry. Connor always apologized after they'd had sex during his Kamirth. She knew he felt bad that he was unable to control his actions and always worried about hurting her.

As the elevator started upward once again, Jenna smiled. If things remained as they always had, Connor would want sex again, but this time it would be slow and sweet. His attention directed toward her pleasure. When the doors opened, a couple stepped aside so Connor and Jenna could exit. She was certain by the looks they received, it was obvious what had gone on inside a stuck elevator.

Connor led her to the end of the hall. "It should be quiet down here." He tapped his card on the reader and opened the door. The room was spacious for a hotel with a king bed and a small sitting area with a blue loveseat, matching chair, and a desk. There was a wooden hutch that held a single serve coffeemaker and a mini fridge.

"Nice." Jenna plopped onto the bed. "You know I don't have any clothes. Not even a toothbrush." Connor paced the room, suddenly making it feel cramped.

"I'll take you to get some things at your place later. Will that work?"

"Sure." She leaned back on a stack of pillows and watched as he pulled out his laptop and placed it on the desk. He was looking for the file that would have been sent to him regarding the other deaths. After several tense minutes, he finally looked up from his screen.

"Those girls died exactly the same way as Sarah." He rested his forehead in his palms. "I detected nothing at the scene other than the gasoline used to start the blaze."

Jenna felt the emotions roll off of him. Connor didn't take kindly to failure. No dragon did. Being enhanced, they were good at most everything they did, and they thrived on a sense of accomplishment. It was rare a dragon gave up on a task. It simply wasn't programed into their DNA.

A burning question hung in the air. "Were they also banned by the elders?"

He finally lifted his head. Brown eyes, a mixture of amber and green with anger, met hers. "One was, the other was betrothed. Her mate was away fighting a brush fire."

Her chest tightened. "I can't imagine."

He shoved back the chair with such force it rolled into the curtains before stopping. In two strides, he stood beside the bed. A growl rumbled low in his chest. "I thought I died when you left me, but that was nothing compared to how I would feel if something happened to you."

She sat up and licked her lips. "You never once told me you loved me. Why?"

"I wish I had an answer. I'm an idiot and I guess I assumed you knew." The mattress dipped from his weight as he sat beside her, his hand on her thigh. "Tell me what I need to do to make this work between us, because I can't let you walk away again. Do I need to move to Dallas? I hate this climate, but I'll do anything that makes you happy."

She appreciated his honesty and couldn't lie any longer. "I wasn't entirely truthful earlier."

He arched a brow.

"I still love you. Every day here has been a challenge. I've tried to forget about you, but you're kinda unforgettable." This time he waggled his brows and she giggled. Something she realized she hadn't done much of in a long time.

"You swear no matter what, we'll always be together?" He'd told her so before, but she needed to hear it again.

He pulled her hand into his. "Nothing and no one can come between us. I don't care about anything except you. We can be the first to work at making change. Let others see we're together because we love each other."

She smiled. "I like that." His grin went from ear to ear. God, he was handsome, and he was hers.

"Sooo, not that I'm trying to be pushy, but when can we finish the mating? When can I officially make you mine?"

"Not here and not back home. There are too many bad memories in both places." Jenna tapped her index finger on her lips. "Can we go someplace special?"

"Any place you want, baby. Name it." He drew her hand to his lips and gave a soft kiss to her knuckles.

"I've always wanted to visit Denali."

His mouth dropped open but was quickly replaced by a wicked grin. "I happen to know a perfect little cave that's off limits to any humans. I could take you flying at night, and we could watch the Northern lights. As soon as I finish the investigation here, we'll go."

"It sounds perfect. I can't wait."

He leaned in and kissed her. It started as a slow, soft caress on her lips then turned into a demand for more. He backed away, leaving her breathless.

"I have to go, but we will finish this later."

She couldn't wait.

13

Connor headed out, leaving Jenna in the room to get some much needed sleep. He'd talked to O'Donnell and decided to meet him at the police station. The attorney had assured him Jenna would be cleared of any suspicion, so he kissed her and promised to take her home for some of her things when he returned. In the meantime, she would stay with him until they figured out what was going on with these arsons.

"Well, I would have to say after looking over these files, that it's definitely the same perp," Ethan commented, looking over the top of the manila folder at Connor.

He sat across from the detective's desk, deep in thought of Jenna in his bed, which was where he really wanted to be right now. "I would have to say the dragons are a target, but I'm confused by the other unrelated fires you've had here. If my people are who the bastard's after, why burn those other buildings?"

The detective shook his head. "Good question and I wish I had the answer. Your people on either scene didn't detect anything?"

"No, and that has me even more worried. Whoever it is, is good at covering their tracks. I'll be doing a conference call later tonight with the others who were on the out of state scenes, just so we can compare notes."

Ethan set the folder on his desk. "I hope you find something,"—the phone rang—"Excuse me." He grabbed his cell. "Yeah."

Tension coiled through the air as Ethan sat forward in his chair, his body stiff. Connor knew they had another fire on their hands, and he hoped to hell there were no casualties this time.

Ethan looked up. "They have no idea if it's our guy, but the hotel you're staying at is on fire."

Connor shot from his seat. "Everyone get out?" he yelled as he ran out the office and down the hall. Skirting past the desks, the other officers got out of his way.

"I'm not sure. They've called for backup." Ethan was right behind him as they both hit the parking lot. Panic strung every nerve tight. The thought of losing Jenna made him ill.

"Stand back! I'm going to shift." There was no way Connor would make the drive across town. Fuck the rules. He'd always hated them anyway.

Bone snapped as he decided on a small sleek dragon. It would be easier to navigate the skyscrapers. He hardly noticed Ethan's face, which contorted into a mixture of surprise and awe. A female in the lot let out a scream. Within seconds, he stood three feet tall with a wingspan that almost doubled his height. He stretched the appendages he hadn't felt in a long time and gave a flap to try them out. He usually preferred his primary form, which was a much larger size, but small was necessary at the moment. With the detective yelling something unintelligible, and another guy in a designer suit running toward them, Connor sprang into the air. He watched Ethan and the attorney run for his car, Ethan tossing out some colorful words the entire way.

Jenna? His dragon reached out for its mate. He screeched in fear when she didn't reply and rocketed through the air. *Jenna, baby I'm coming. Please hang on.* Sheer terror pushed him to fly faster. He was a flash that sped by. An apparition to many who shook their heads, believing they were seeing things. He caught a current that sent him higher and helped move him closer to the woman he loved more than anything. He'd die for her, and right now, he was kicking himself because he had let his ego, his pride, and his stubbornness get the better of him. He should have searched for her the moment he'd read the note and demanded she come back to him.

Yeah, that would have gone over like a bag full of scorpions. He also should have told her how he felt long ago. Maybe she wouldn't have felt the need to flee.

Smoke rose thick and black in the distance, and his heart nearly stopped. He swore he saw a finger curl through the blackness and beckon him. He narrowed his gaze and headed straight for it. As he approached, he bore witness to the horrors the firefighters battled. Flames climbed up the side of the building from the main, third and fifth floors. Every couple of floors appeared to be ablaze. No way could this be the work of one person. How the hell would they have gotten out? Hadn't the sprinklers worked?

He scanned the crowd that stood around the several ambulances on the scene. Opening his senses, there was no detection of Jenna. His worst fear was met.

She was still inside.

Jenna?

Still no response. He summoned all the magic at his disposal. Searching for her life force, he flew to the other side of the building where his room was located. The tenth floor was engulfed. Fear gripped him tighter as he finally found Jenna's faint heartbeat.

So slow. She was on the brink of death.

He raced to the window, hovered, and realized the glass was still intact. People shouted from below, but he paid no attention. In his dragon form, he could withstand the smoke and fire. Even if it destroyed him, he would go in anyway.

Circling back, he picked up speed, folded his wings against his body to help protect them, and crashed through the thick pane of glass. Shards cut into his skin and a warm wetness trickled between his eyes and down his sides. He somersaulted into the room, crashing into the desk before he stopped with a grunt. Standing, he shook off chunks of glass and let his vision adjust. Even with excellent sight, he still had difficulty seeing through the thick mass of smoke. Fire hadn't found its way into the room yet, but the toxin-filled air was enough to kill any human.

Jenna's heart stopped.

No!

He shifted back and felt his way to the bed where he found her limp body. Her hands were tied behind her back, and she lay on her stomach. He gently scooped her up and headed for the window. With her body tucked to his chest, he leaped to the sill and jumped. He willed all his magic to his wings and made a partial shift, so he could still keep hold of her, yet fly gently to the ground. When he landed near the crew administering first aid, he laid her down. Two men came running with an oxygen tank in hand. Their eyes fixed on his wings.

He produced a claw and cut the bindings around her wrist then rolled her to her back. By all human standards, she was dead. Her lungs were seized from too much smoke and her heart still.

"You do not have my permission to leave," he whispered. Tears stung his eyes.

"Jesus. We have to start CPR," a paramedic said next to him.

Connor growled. "You will not touch her until I say so." He placed both palms on her chest above her breasts. He spread his wings and gave them a slow gentle sweep up and down. Magic spilled around him and cocooned them both in its silky embrace. Words spilled from his lips in the ancient Celtic language as if he had spoken them a hundred times.

"Love of my life. Guardian of my soul. I willingly give you everything I am. My heart, my magic, and my very essence." Power flared into a light so white it nearly blinded him. The men beside him shielded their eyes.

"My breath is your breath. With every beat of my heart, yours will follow. My tears..." He completely shifted into his primary dragon. A sleek, yet muscular black beast that towered over his petite mate.

The two paramedics scooted backward.

Connor's power flared from white to cobalt blue. "My tears flow and bring the beginning of life." A single drop fell and touched her cheek.

Jenna floated and watched as the big onyx dragon bent over her. Seeing herself on the ground was more than a bit strange. But the peace, which swept over her and wrapped her in a warm and loving embrace, had her quickly forgetting the scene below. She drifted backward toward a calming bliss, when she suddenly stopped. A tear slipped from the dragon's eye and it wrenched at her. How had she not noticed the beauty of the beast before? Its skin so black; it shimmered like a mirror. Muscles, firm and strong, filled out its body, yet the dragon was sleek. She instinctively knew he was powerful but gentle. His tear touched her face, and she drew in a breath.

Connor.

Recognition struck, and she battled with the peace that surrounded her and a burning desire to go back to him. She was part of the dragon. He needed her and she needed him.

Searing pain burned her chest. She tried to gasp for air, but her lungs refused to cooperate. Slowly, she forced her eyes open and met a pair of almond-shaped green eyes surrounded by a large head. The dragon's nose came within inches of her own and exhaled. The scent of spice and chocolate surrounded her and sent air rushing to fill her lungs. She clutched the earth beneath her, ripping at it as tears slipped down the side of her face, the pain so severe.

The dragon morphed into a man. His eyes glistened as he cupped her face. "I know it hurts, but you have to exhale."

She stared into the depths of those cocoa eyes and forced the air from her lungs.

"Good girl. Follow my lead." He inhaled a deep breath. She forced her lungs to cooperate and dragged in a rattling breath. It was as if she were drowning. Her lungs were filled with foreign material, and there was no room for air. She was suffocating but remained focused on his gaze. Again, they exhaled together and this time she went into a coughing rage. After what felt like minutes, she calmed and noticed the pain was gone. She was breathing much easier. Connor spoke to someone.

"Now you can give her oxygen. Check her vitals." He began to move away, and she tried to reach out as someone put a mask over her face.

"Shhh. Don't struggle." He stroked her hair.

She shoved the paramedic's hand away and lifted the mask, her senses finally intact. "You need to help save the others. I'll be fine now." She knew Connor wouldn't want to leave her, but neither could he let the others perish. He kissed her forehead.

"I'll go." Then he looked at the man attending her. "You let anything happen to her and I'll kill you."

"Connor!" A man yelled.

Jenna recognized Detective Collins as he filled her vision. He appeared out of breath and had another gentleman with him.

"Ethan. Stay here and guard my mate. Shoot anyone who looks suspicious," Connor growled before he shifted and flew away back into the inferno.

The detective looked down at her. "How are you doing?"

"I'd say considering she was dead only moments ago, pretty damn good." Jenna finally realized it was Trent who spoke as he slapped a blood pressure cuff to her arm. She was relieved to be in excellent hands.

"Damn, Jenna. I've never seen anything like it in my life. Flying dragons, magic voodoo shit, and bringing back the dead." He smiled at her. "Please tell me you don't have a craving for flesh or human brains."

She laughed and pushed herself up, freeing the mask from her face.

"Hey." Trent started to admonish her but she held up a hand.

"I'm fine. Really." She stared at the hotel, which finally looked like it was relenting to the tons of water being dumped on it. "Connor is very powerful. He brought me back." And broke a huge rule in the process. Shifting in front of humans, no matter the reason, was not tolerated. He could be banned from the clan and his position in the firefighting crew stripped. Also, using magic where others could see. Yeah, he was in some serious shit, but as she watched him fly across the smoke-filled sky, she knew he didn't care. Fire was his mistress and saving people and property his life. He'd find a way to move on.

She caught the gaze of another. Derrick, covered in soot, worked in the distance. She wanted to go to him, but this wasn't the time. Later, she would tell him everything. The man in the suit knelt in front of her.

"Miss Dunne? I'm Patrick O'Donnell, District Council attorney. I'm happy to see you're safe." He handed her his card. "We can talk later. I'm going to snoop around."

She accepted the piece of paper. "Thank you, Mr. O'Donnell."

14

Connor flew through the hallway on the top floor of the hotel. Still shaken after losing Jenna, he hadn't been sure if he could bring her back. After all, they were not completely mated yet. A minor fact he intended to correct right away. Thankfully, his power was stronger than even he had realized.

Opening his senses, he detected no humans and moved to the next floor. He could hear the muffled sounds of the firefighters who searched the smoke-filled corridors below, and he tried to make his way closer. As he moved down to the next floor, the smoke was so thick even he had difficulty seeing. He heard them say the fire was under control, but they were worried about casualties. Conditions were less than ideal, but it was still possible for survivors. His dragon was in its element, even though it hated the searing heat.

He detected several men ahead; crawling along the corridor, their ability to see would be zero. He landed behind them, folded in his wings, and summoned a larger form. Once he'd grown and filled the hall, he took in a deep breath and released it in a slow steady stream of air that pushed the smoke away. It wasn't completely clear, but it was enough they could get to their feet and continue working. The man at the back of the line turned and gave Connor a salute.

He nodded then shrunk enough to take flight again, thinking that this is how it should have been all along. Shifters held special abilities when in their dragon form; magic was helpful in saving lives. Yet, the elders refused to allow the use of either in the presence of humanity. Screw it. Things needed to change, and with Jenna by his side, they would change them together.

Escaping out a broken window, he flew around the outside of the building. Jenna was sitting up and looking into the sky, watching him. People on the ground pointed, but none seemed overly afraid. He banked to the right and angled around the front when something caught his attention. A scent. Something he hadn't detected before. Now for some reason, it burst through the air, and he knew exactly who it belonged to.

An ancient. One skilled in masking both scent and physical form. But why? He intended to find out and quickly made his way back into the building. Following the scent to the bowels of the hotel, he ended up in the basement. It didn't take long for the one he was chasing to make an appearance.

"You should have stayed at home." An elder by the name of Cyrus stepped from the still lingering smoke.

"What are you doing here?" Connor had shifted back to human form and contemplated his next move. The shifter in front of him had a few thousand years on Connor and was therefore much more powerful.

"Doing what should have been done long ago. These females are a waste of resources and need to be purged from society." Cyrus took a step closer, but Connor held his ground. No way in hell was he backing down.

"What resources? You ban them from our society, so they go and live with the humans. How does that hurt us?" Connor's anger grew when he thought about the deaths this man had caused.

Cyrus laughed. "You are a fool if you believe that. They are of no use to us in the breeding program. They mix our DNA with the humans, creating useless mutts that are allowed to wander around. Who knows how far this mess has spread."

The asshole was crazy. "Breeding? Is that all you're concerned about?" He curled his fingers into his palms. Somehow, he had to subdue Cyrus and get him out of here...but to where? "How many of the elders are in on this little extermination of yours?" He had to buy some time. Somehow distract him so he could reach for the dagger in his boot. The blade was coated with diamond dust. When shoved into a dragon, it would either keep him from shifting or force him to shift back. Connor would figure out what to do with him later. Maybe local authorities could help get him on a plane headed back to Minnesota.

"You should make breeding your number one concern as well. Our species will one day be extinct if we don't become more diligent." Cyrus seemed to relax, likely confident Connor couldn't harm him. "I've been encouraging the other elders to form a law that will demand all males take two mates. Every female of age should be bred."

Connor's temper simmered. *Keep him talking so you can make your move.* "Then why did you try to kill my mate?"

The older dragon leaned against the wall and crossed his arms over his chest. "She is a halfling, an abomination. Our race must stay pure."

He really was fucked up in the head. Every female born to a mated couple was a precious gift, including the ones who couldn't bear shifter children themselves. They were family, no matter what. Connor shifted his weight, lowered his head, and barreled forward. When his head came into contact with Cyrus's gut, he reached into his boot and withdrew the dagger. With a quick thrust, he embedded it into Cyrus's thigh. Not the ideal spot, but it would do for now.

The shifter roared and punched Connor in the neck before Connor wrapped him in a vice and jerked. Vertebrae snapped and Connor was thankful to be a quick healer. His fingers still wrapped around the dagger, he gave it a twist, forcing Cyrus to release him. Once free, he fisted his other hand and landed an upper cut under Cyrus's jaw, causing the shifters head to snap back and hit the wall behind Cyrus.

"Seize him," a strong female voice commanded.

By then, Connor had Cyrus by the throat and turned his head to see Rosalee, one of the oldest females in the clan, storming toward them with three soldiers surrounding her. She stopped next to Connor.

"We will take him home and he will face death," she stated calmly.

The men threw diamond-covered shackles on Cyrus's wrists, neck, and ankles. One pulled the dagger from the shifter's thigh and handed it back to Connor. He accepted it and wiped the blood on his jeans before seating it back into his boot.

"What the hell is going on? You knew what he was doing?" Connor tried to hide the edge in his tone and remember who he was speaking to. Damn, but he didn't care anymore. "He tried to kill my mate!"

Rosalee touched his arm. "I know and for that I am sorry. I'm grateful you were able to bring her back. We've been tracking Cyrus and trying to catch him in the act, but he always remained one step ahead of us."

"People died," Connor snarled. "Why didn't you warn us?"

Rosalee's blonde brow arched high. "And have him realize we were on to him? I never meant for people to die, but Cyrus is the oldest among us. Having patience was the only way to catch him."

Connor knew she spoke the truth, but it tasted like shit and he didn't like it. "Things need to change." He pulled his shoulders back. "Things will change."

This time she granted him a smile. "It is past time, Connor, but your breaking our laws will not help."

"It was necessary and I would do it again." He was not sorry in the least, and it was time the elders realized how wrong they were.

A twinkle sparked in her eyes. "You are what the future needs. Both you and your mate will have a seat on the council and help us bring our people into the current century."

"You offer me a seat rather than punish my disobedience?"

Her gaze turned fierce. "If only more males would display their true feelings, we might be in a better place. What you did was for the woman you love, and I applaud that not punish it."

"Then I am honored." He bowed his head in respect.

She turned and walked away, blending into the lingering smoke until she was gone. He wiped his brow. Was it finally over? He had to reach Jenna and reassure himself she was still okay.

Connor led Jenna down a narrow passage. "Keep hold of my hand. It can be slick through here." He glanced back to be sure she was okay and was greeted by a wide smile and a pair of sparkling hazel eyes. God, how he loved this woman and could hardly believe she was his. They were about to complete the final phase of their bond. She would be with him for as long as he lived, and even if they didn't have children of their own, he didn't care. As long as they were together, that was all he needed. There were a lot of children in the world who needed parents, and both he and Jenna had a lot of love to give.

"Do you really think the elders are going to make changes?" Jenna asked.

"Rosalee seemed genuine when she talked to me. Cyrus will have his head taken for his crimes." He stopped and brought her hand to his lips, pressing a kiss to her knuckles. "I'm sorry. It doesn't bring back Sarah."

She nodded. "At least he won't be able to hurt anyone else." She smiled. "This is about us. From this day forward, we start a life together. No more talk about the past and no regrets. It's a new beginning."

"I love you."

"I love you too." She laughed. "Now, how much further?"

"Almost there." He couldn't wait for her approval when she saw where they were going and pressed forward. As they rounded the next bend, he heard her gasp. He pulled her forward to stand in front of him. Clutching her to his chest, he kissed the top of her head. "Do you like it?"

"Oh, Connor it's... It's unreal. Like something you'd expect to see in a fantasy movie."

"I take it you approve?" He stared over the top of her head. The cavern popped with vivid purple and red and a turquoise center, where a deep pool demanded they strip and take a dip. Temperatures were a cool fifty-five, perfect for them.

She turned to face him. "I approve." Hunger burned in her gaze as she licked her lips. "You have too many clothes on."

His cock stirred.

"I'm sure you know how to rectify that."

She flashed a wicked grin and reached for the hem of her sweater. With painstaking slowness, she pulled it up. The pink knit slid past her taut stomach and stopped just beneath her ribs. Her grin grew wider. "Perhaps this is a bad idea," she teased.

He growled, his erection already painful against his jeans. "The only idea that will prove bad is you hesitating much longer. If you like that sweater, then you'd best remove it before I rip it from your body."

The amber in her eyes deepened and defiance flashed before she pulled the sweater free and gave him a view of full, round breasts. His gaze took in every curve down to the jeans that sat on her hips. "Now the pants, angel."

She shoved her thumbs into the belt loops and cocked a hip to the side. "In a hurry?"

"You're a vixen, you know that? Just remember I can tease you until you beg me to let you come." He lifted a brow. "And beg you will."

Her eyes widened, and she made quick work of the button and zipper. Before he could exhale, her jeans were off and she was headed for the water. Diving in, she broke the stillness of the serene pool and disappeared under the surface. Seconds later, she came up. Blonde hair slicked back, her breasts seeming to float on the water. All resolve was lost and he tore at his clothes.

Jenna nibbled her lip as she watched Connor pull the gray tee over his head. Her tongue begged to lick every peak and valley across his chest. The man gave a pair of jeans a life of their own. He moved like a predator and when he pinned his gaze on her, she knew he intended to devour her.

She shuddered.

He was male perfection. Powerful, lethal, a force to be reckoned with. He was a centuries-old dragon, and he was going to make her his.

Strong hands pushed his jeans past powerful thighs. His erection stood to full attention, and she licked her lips.

"Now who is the tease?" she questioned.

With a quick kick, he had his pants on the other side of the cavern and was in the water making a beeline for her. She squealed and tried to swim away, but he grabbed her ankle and pulled her under. With his hands on her waist, he pushed her to the surface.

"Trying to run, angel?" His eyes gleamed with mischief, and she knew she was in for a treat.

"Not me."

His fingers traced a line along her collarbone then followed the top of her breasts until both hands were cupping them. He rolled her nipples between his fingers.

"Oh, Conn––."

His mouth came down on hers. Tongue, searing hot, swept in and tasted every inch of her mouth. Flames licked at her core; she clawed his back and wrapped her legs around his waist in an attempt to rub against his erection.

He broke free and she moaned.

"Don't worry. I intend to take real good care of you." Once again, he gripped her by the waist and this time carried her to the water's edge where he set her up on a smooth rock. The look of hunger in his eyes as he spread her thighs caused her nipples to harden. She leaned back slightly, and he laved his tongue along her folds, teasing as his hot breath blew over her clit.

"Stop teasing. You owe me," she whispered. Damn, she needed release. He must have agreed because he slid his tongue over her nub then sucked. She curled her fingers and tried to grab hold, but couldn't gain purchase on the rock beneath her. Instead, she slipped them into his thick hair and held his head to her. No way was she letting go until he gave her what she needed.

He inserted one finger then two between her folds and teased as he gave a light nip, sending the bundle of nerves in her clit into a frenzy. She was on the edge. Waiting––no begging to fall. Not caring if there was anyone there to catch her.

With a twist of his wrist, he buried his fingers, pulled them out then pushed deep again with increasing speed.

She dug her nails into his scalp as her orgasm hung just out of reach. Every muscle in her legs tightened, and she arched her back. Finally, release swept over her, ripping a cry from her lips as she shattered into a million pieces.

Connor didn't stop. He continued swirling his tongue, lapping and sucking until he wrung another orgasm from her. When he pulled back, he gazed at her with a devilish grin on his face.

"I'm not done with you yet." He lifted her off the rock and set her in the water in front of him. The coolness helped ease the heat that burned inside her. He lifted her. "Wrap your legs around me."

She didn't need to be told twice. Once she'd locked herself around his waist, he teased her opening with the head of his cock. Pushing in slightly, making her want more. She tried to take all of him, but he held her firm.

Two can play this game. Jenna pressed her fingers into his shoulders and leaned closer. Nipped at his bottom lip then suckled before she kissed him. Thrust her tongue into his mouth and put forth all the passion she felt. Pressing her breasts against his chest didn't hurt either. Within seconds, he thrust his hips and seated himself fully inside her.

They moaned in unison.

She broke the kiss. "Make me yours," she whispered against his mouth.

He pumped faster and in a flash, his fangs were buried in her shoulder. Venom rushed into her bloodstream as magic slid around them. Silent words, whispered in Connor's mind, bound them together. As their pleasure peaked and release shattered both their bodies, she felt a stir deep inside her. Their heartbeats became one. Every breath she took matched his. Their souls connected. She would live as long as her mate lived. His power would increase her own.

"How do you feel?" He looked her over with concern. "Do you feel it? Us?"

"I do. It's like you're part of me now. I feel like a piece of me has been missing, and now I'm whole again."

He kissed her forehead and pulled free, setting her on her feet. "Today we start a new life. When we go back home, it will be to show our people that change is good. It may take time, but it will happen."

She was excited about their new life together and confident their people would embrace change. The future of the shifter and human race would benefit. Most important, Connor would still be able to do what he loved most. Fire was his mistress, and it had shaped the man she had grown to love.

EPILOGUE

Derrick sat on the bench and stared into his locker. The fire had nearly kicked their ass, but they had managed. His crew, and the others called in from the surrounding area, had all left alive. The hotel staff and patrons had also managed to flee with little more than bruises and smoke inhalation. He nearly died though when he saw Jenna, lying still on the ground.

"Hey."

He turned his head toward the soft voice.

"Hey. How are you feeling?"

Jenna smiled. "Good."

He looked down at the towel in his hands. "I heard you died. That Connor was able to bring you back." He gazed at her from the corner of his eye. "It's all the talk here."

She sat down beside him. "Yes, he did."

"I'm glad. I was worried about you when I saw..." He couldn't finish the words. Her lifeless body haunted him.

"I came to apologize. I never got over Connor, and it was wrong of me to allow you to think we had a chance." He felt her warm touch on his shoulder. "I hope one day you can forgive me. I never meant to hurt you."

He stood, shaking off her grip. "Sure, Jenna. I understand." Like hell he did. Would it have made a difference if he had made his move sooner? The moment she'd walked into his station he'd fallen. The more he got to know her and her kind nature, the more he thought she was the woman for him. How wrong he had been. Still, he wished her all the happiness even if he wasn't the one to give it to her.

"So will you be staying on here?"

"No. Connor and I have been invited to sit on the council, which resides in the motherland."

He exhaled. At least she wouldn't be here. "Where's that?"

"Ireland."

Even better. She'd be farther away and hopefully easier to forget. "What about your house and the coffee shop?" He wasn't sure why he was inclined to ask. Maybe he just needed to keep her near him.

"I'm giving the house to Kate and as for the shop... Well I'm donating it to the local woman's shelter. I hope it will serve to help many of them get back on their feet."

He had to look at her. See those hazel eyes one more time. "That's a good thing you're doing."

"Thanks." She stood. "I guess I should be going. I wish you all the best, Derrick. Someday the perfect girl will come along, and she will love you with all her heart." She leaned in and pressed a quick kiss to his cheek then rushed out the door.

Gone. In a flash, the one woman he'd thought the perfect fit had just shattered his heart.

ABOUT THE AUTHOR

Award winning and bestselling author Valerie Twombly grew up watching Dark Shadows over her mother's shoulder, and from there her love of the fanged creatures blossomed. Today, Valerie has decided to take her darker, sensual side and put it to paper. When she is not busy creating a world full of steamy, hot men and strong, seductive women, she juggles her time between a full-time job, hubby and her German Shepherd dog, in Northern IL. Valerie is a member of Romance Writers of America and Fantasy, Futuristic and Paranormal Romance Writers.

Sign up for Valerie's newsletter and be the first to hear about new releases, receive special excerpts and exclusive contests. http://valerietwombly.com/newsletter-sign/

Follow Valerie
www.valerietwombly.com

ALSO BY VALERIE TWOMBLY

Visit ValerieTwombly.Com

An Angel's Torment (Eternally Mated Prequel)

Fall Into Darkness (Eternally Mated #1)

Veiled In Darkness (Eternally Mated #2)

Bound By Darkness (Eternally Mated #3)

Unleash The Darkness (Eternally Mated #4)

Surrender To Darkness (Eternally Mated #5)

Tempted By Darkness (Eternally Mated #6)

Spanish Nights, A Jinn's Seduction

Sultry Nights, A Jinn's Seduction

Taken By Desire (Demonic Desires #1)

Taken By Storm (Demonic Desires #2)

Passion Awakened (Beyond The Mist)

Rescue Me (Sparks Of Desire)

www.ingramcontent.com/pod-product-compliance
Lightning Source LLC
LaVergne TN
LVHW091933070526
838200LV00068B/970